CATE TIERNAN

WICCA

SPELLBOUND

The sixth book in the series

PUFFIN BOOKS

PUFFIN BOOKS

Published by the Penguin Group
Penguin Books Ltd, 80 Strand, London WC2R 0RL, England
Penguin Putnam Inc., 375 Hudson Street, New York, New York 10014, USA
Penguin Books Australia Ltd, 250 Camberwell Road, Camberwell, Victoria 3124, Australia
Penguin Books Canada Ltd, 10 Alcorn Avenue, Toronto, Ontario, Canada M4V 3B2
Penguin Books India (P) Ltd, 11 Community Centre, Panchsheel Park, New Delhi – 110 017, India
Penguin Books (NZ) Ltd, Cnr Rosedale and Airborne Roads, Albany, Auckland, New Zealand
Penguin Books (South Africa) (Pty) Ltd, 24 Sturdee Avenue, Rosebank 2196, South Africa

Penguin Books Ltd, Registered Offices: 80 Strand, London WC2R 0RL, England

www.penguin.com

First published in the USA in Puffin Books, a division of Penguin Putnam Books for Young Readers,
2001
Published in Great Britain in Puffin Books 2002
6

Copyright © 17th Street Productions, an Alloy Online, Inc. company, 2001
All rights reserved

17th Street Productions and associated logos
are trademarks and/or registered trademarks of Alloy Online, Inc.

All quoted materials in this work were created by the author
Any resemblance to existing works is accidental

Printed in England by Clays Ltd, St Ives plc

British Library Cataloguing in Publication Data
A CIP catalogue record for this book is available from the British Library

ISBN 0–141–31405–2

1.
Kithic

Beltane, 1962, San Francisco

Today I met my future, and I'm dancing on sunlight!
This A.M. I celebrated Beltane in the park downtown, and
all of us from Catspaw made beautiful magick right there
in the open while people watched. The sun was shining, we
wore flowers in our hair, and we wove our ribbons around the
fertility pole and made music and raised a power that
filled everything with light. We had elderflower wine, and
everything was so open and beautiful. The Goddess was in
me, her life force, and I was awed by my own power.

I knew then that I was ready to be with a man — I'm
seventeen and a woman. And as soon as I had that
thought, I looked up into someone's eyes. Stella Laban was
giving him a paper cup of wine, and he took it and sipped,
and my knees almost buckled at the sight of his lips.

Stella introduced us. His name is Patrick, and he's from Seattle. His coven is Waterwind. So he's Woodbane, like me, like all of Catspaw.

I couldn't stop looking at him. I noticed that his chestnut brown hair was shot through with gray, and he had laugh lines around his eyes. He was older than I thought, much older, maybe even fifty.

Then he smiled at me, and I felt my heart thud to a stop. Someone grabbed Stella around the waist, and she danced off, laughing. Patrick held out his hand, and without thinking I put mine in his and he led me away from the group. We sat on a boulder, the sun warm on my bare shoulders, and talked forever. When he stood up, I followed him to his car.

Now we're at his house, and he's sleeping, and I am so, so happy. When he wakes up, I'll say two things: I love you. Teach me everything.

—SB

I had been to Sharon Goodfine's house once before, with Bree Warren, back when Bree and I were best friends. Tonight Sharon was hosting Cirrus's usual Saturday-night circle, and I was curious to see how it would feel different from other circles we'd had. Each place had its own feeling, its own atmosphere. Every circle was different.

"Nice pad," said Robbie Gurevitch, my other best friend from childhood. He squinted at the landscape lighting, the manicured shrubs with their caps of snow, the white-painted brick of the colonial house. The landscaping alone probably cost more than what my dad makes in a year at IBM. Sharon's dad was an orthodontist with a bunch of famous clients. I'd heard a rumor that he'd straightened Justin Timberlake's teeth.

"Yep," I answered, pushing my hands into my pockets and starting up the walk. I'd gotten a ride with Robbie in his red Beetle, and I saw other cars I recognized, parked along the wide street. Jenna Ruiz was here. Matt Adler had come in his own car, of course, since he and Jenna were broken up. Ethan Sharp was here. Hunter was here, I noticed. I shivered inside my coat with a blend of excitement and dread. More cars were parked nearby, but I didn't recognize them and figured one of the neighbors was having a party.

On the porch Robbie stopped me as I started to ring the doorbell. I looked at him questioningly.

"You okay?" he asked quietly, his gray-blue eyes dark.

I opened my mouth to indignantly say, "Of course," but then I shut it again. I'd known Robbie too long and had been through too much with him to fob him off with white lies. He had been one of the first people I'd told about being a blood witch, about being adopted, about being Woodbane. Of the seven Great Clans of Wicca, Woodbanes were the ones who sought power at all costs, the ones who worked with dark magick. When I'd found out about being a blood witch, I hadn't known my clan and had hoped that I was a Rowanwand, a Wyndenkell, a Brightendale, a Burnhide. Even a mischievous Leapvaughn or warlike Vikroth would have been fine. But no. I was Woodbane: tainted.

Robbie and Bree had saved my life three weeks ago, when

Cal, the guy I'd loved, had tried to kill me. And Robbie's friendship had helped give me the strength to continue searching for the truth about my birth parents. He could read me well, and he knew I was feeling fragile right now.

So I just said, "Well, I'm hoping the circle will help."

He nodded, satisfied, and I rang the doorbell.

"Hi!" Sharon said, opening the door wide and ushering us in, the perfect hostess. I caught sight of Jenna and Ethan standing behind her, talking. "Dump your coats in the living room. I've set up a space in the media room. Hunter told me we'd have a real crowd tonight, and he was right." She pointed to a doorway on the far side of the large living room. Her fine, dark hair swirled around her shoulders as she turned to answer a question from Jenna. Her trademark gold bracelets jangled.

I was standing there, wondering how small the room must be if the seven members of Cirrus would crowd it, when Robbie caught my eye. "Media room?" he mouthed silently, shrugging out of his coat. I couldn't help smiling.

Then I felt a prickle of awareness at the back of my neck, and knowing what it meant, I looked around to see Hunter Niall coming purposefully toward me. The rest of the room faded, and I suddenly heard my own heartbeat loud in my ears. I was only vaguely aware of Robbie walking away to greet someone.

"You've been avoiding me," Hunter said softly in his English accent.

"Yes," I admitted, looking into his sea green eyes. I knew he'd called my house at least twice since the last time we'd seen each other, but I hadn't returned his calls.

He leaned back against the door frame. I was five-six, and Hunter was a good seven inches taller than me. I hadn't seen him since a few days ago, when I'd had witnessed him stripping one of my friends of his magickal powers. He'd done it because it was his job. As a Seeker and the youngest member of the International Council of Witches, Hunter had been obligated to wrest David Redstone's power from him and to bind him magickally so that he couldn't use magick again for any reason. It had been like watching someone being tortured, and I'd had trouble sleeping since then.

But that wasn't all. Hunter and I had kissed the night before the ritual, and I'd felt a longing for him that astonished and disturbed me. Then, after the ritual, Hunter had given me a spelled crystal into which he'd put his own image, through the sheer power of his feelings. We both knew there was something between us, something that might be incredibly powerful, but we hadn't explored it yet. I both wanted to and didn't want to. I was drawn to him, but what he had done still frightened me. Unable to sort out my own feelings, I'd resorted to a tried-and-true tactic: avoidance.

"I'm glad you came tonight," he said, and his voice seemed to smooth away some of my tension. "Morgan," he added, sounding uncharacteristically hesitant. "It was a hard thing you saw. It's a hard thing to be part of. It was the third one I've done, and it only gets harder each time. But the council decreed it, and it was necessary. You know what happened to Stuart Afton."

"Yes," I said quietly. Stuart Afton, a local businessman, was still recovering from the stroke David Redstone had caused by working a dark spell. Now David was in Ireland, at a hospice run by a Brightendale coven. He would live there for a long time, learning how to exist without magick.

"You know, some people join Wicca or are born into it, and it's more or less smooth sailing," Hunter went on. Ethan passed us on the way to the media room, and I heard the fizzy pop of someone opening a soda can. Hunter lowered his voice, and the two of us were alone in our conversation. "They study for years, they work magick, and it's all just a calm acknowledgment of the cycle, the circle, the life wheel."

I heard a burst of laughter from the media room. I glanced over Hunter's shoulder, catching a glimpse of a boy I almost recognized. He wasn't part of our coven, and I wondered why he was here.

Hunter was making me nervous, jumpy, as he often did— he had always affected me strongly, and I didn't understand our connection any more than I understood the surprising, even frightening attraction I had to him.

"Yes?" I said, trying to follow his thought.

"With you," he went on, "it hasn't been a smooth ride. Wicca and everything associated with it has been one huge trauma after another. Your birth mother, Belwicket, the dark wave, Cal, Selene, now David . . . You haven't had much of a chance to revel in magick's beauty, to appreciate the joy that comes from working a perfect spell, to experience the excitement of learning, finding out more and more. . . ."

I nodded, looking at him. My feelings about him had changed so radically, so fast. I'd hated him when I met him. Now he seemed so compelling and attractive and in tune with me. What was that about? Had he changed, or had I?

Hunter straightened his shoulders. "All I'm saying is,

you've had a hard time, a hard autumn, and so far a hard winter. Magick can help you. I can help you—if you'll let me." Then he turned and went to the media room as I gazed after him, and a moment later the voices quieted, and I heard Hunter asking for attention.

I peeled off my coat, dropped it on a chair, and went to join the circle.

Sharon's plush media room was indeed crowded. Our coven, Cirrus, consisted of seven members: Hunter, our leader; me, Morgan Rowlands; Jenna; Matt; Sharon; Ethan; Robbie. But there were more than seven people in the room. Next to the big-screen TV, I caught sight of Robbie talking to Bree Warren. Bree—my ex–best friend, then for a while my enemy when we'd fought over Cal. What was she doing at Sharon's house, at our coven meeting? She was a member of Kithic, the rival coven that she'd formed with Raven Meltzer and Hunter's cousin, Sky Eventide.

"Morgan, have you met Simon?" a voice beside me said, and I turned to see Sky herself, motioning to the boy I'd thought I recognized. I realized I'd seen him at a party at Practical Magick, an occult store in the town of Red Kill. The store David Redstone had owned.

"Nice meeting you," Simon said to me.

I blinked. "You too." Turning to Sky, I asked, "What are you guys doing here?"

I was surprised to see a nervous look on Sky's face, which reminded me so much of Hunter's. They were both English; both tall, slender, incredibly blond, somewhat cool and standoffish. They were also both loyal, brave, dedicated to doing what was right. Sky seemed more at ease with people than Hunter did. But Hunter seemed stronger to me.

"Hunter and I have a suggestion," Sky said. "Let's get everyone together, and we'll fill you all in."

"Thank you all for coming," Hunter said, raising his voice. He took a sip of his ginger ale. "We have here two covens," he went on, gesturing around the room. "Cirrus, which has seven members, and Kithic, which has six." He pointed them out to us. "Kithic's leader, Sky Eventide. Bree Warren, Raven Meltzer, Thalia Cutter, Simon Bakehouse, and Alisa Soto."

There was a moment when we were all smiling and nodding at each other, all mystified.

"Hunter and I have been thinking about joining the two covens," said Sky, and I felt my eyebrows raise. When had this discussion happened? I wondered.

Across the room I caught Bree's eye, and she made an I-didn't-know-about-this-either face. Once Bree had been part of Cirrus. Once I had known all her thoughts as well as my own. Well, we were making progress: now we were speaking to each other without fighting, which was more than we'd done for months.

"Each coven is quite small," Hunter explained. "It divides our energy and our powers. If we join, Sky and I can share in the leadership, which will make us stronger."

"And the new coven will have thirteen members," said Sky. "In magick the number thirteen has special properties. A thirteen-member coven will have strength and power. It will make our magick more accessible, for lack of a better word."

"Join?" Jenna asked. Her light brown eyes flitted quickly

to Raven, and I remembered her saying she could never be in the same coven as the girl who had so blatantly stolen Matt away from her. Then her glance fell on Simon, and he looked back at her. I'd seen her talking to him at the Practical Magick party. Well, good for her, I thought. Maybe the lure of Simon would outweigh her feelings about Raven.

"Thirteen sounds really big," said Alisa, who looked young, maybe only fifteen. She had wavy golden brown hair, tan skin, and big dark eyes. "The smaller size is nicer because we know everyone and we can relax with them."

Hunter nodded. "I understand that," he said, and from the tone of his voice I knew he was about to flood her with logic, the way he had done with me so many times. "And I agree that part of a circle's appeal is its intimacy, the sense of closeness and support that we get from one another. But I assure you, after a couple months of working together, we'll appreciate the wider circle of support, the larger group of friends, the greater resource of strength."

Alisa nodded uncertainly.

"Do we get to vote on this?" asked Robbie.

"Yes," Sky said at once. "This is something Hunter and I have thought about a great deal. We share some of the same concerns that you might have. We do think it would be best for the two covens to merge, though, for us to join our energies and strengths. It's what we want to do, how we want to continue on our journey of discovery. But of course, we'd like to hear what the rest of you think."

We were all silent for a moment, everyone waiting for someone else to say something. Then I straightened up. "I think it's a good idea," I said. Until I spoke I wasn't sure what my reaction would be, but now I knew. "It makes sense for us to join together, to be allies, to be working together instead of working apart." Hunter's eyes sought mine, but I looked at the group. "Magick can be dark and dangerous sometimes," I added. "The more people we can count on, the better, in my opinion."

Twelve people looked at me. I had been shy and self-conscious for seventeen years, and I knew that my class-mates, people who knew me well, were surprised at my offering an opinion so openly. But in the last month so much had happened that, frankly, I didn't have a lot of energy left to be self-conscious anymore.

"I agree," Bree said into the silence. I saw the warmth in her brown eyes, and suddenly we smiled at each other, almost as if it were old times.

Everyone started speaking then, and after another twenty minutes of discussion we voted and it was agreed: the two covens would merge. We would be thirteen mem-bers strong, and we would call ourselves Kithic. I hoped the end of Cirrus would help me cope with the traumatic end of Cal's and my relationship. And I tried not to be over-whelmed by all the new beginnings in my life.

We had what I thought of as a "baby" circle: we didn't actually go through the whole ritual, but we did stand in a circle, holding hands, while Hunter and Sky led us through some breathing exercises.

Then Hunter said, "As some of you have already discov-ered, Wicca has its frightening side." He cast a swift look in my direction. "It's not so surprising, perhaps, when you think that all of us have within us the capacity for both bright and dark. Wicca is part of the world, and the world can be a dark place, too. But one of the things this coven can do for you is support you and help you to conquer your personal fears. The fewer unexplored places you have within you, the easier it will be to connect with your own magick."

"We're going to go around the circle," Sky said, picking up where Hunter left off, "and each of us is going to tell the group one of our great fears. Thalia, you start."

Thalia was tall and earth-mothery looking, with long, ringlety hair and a pretty Madonna face (the saint, not the singer).

"I'm afraid of boats," she said, her cheeks turning slightly pink. "Every time I get in a boat, I panic, and I think a whale is going to come up under it and knock me into the sea and I'll drown. Even if it's just a rowboat on a duck pond."

I heard Matt stifle a snicker, and felt a twinge of irritation.

Robbie was next. He looked at Bree, then said, "I'm afraid I won't be patient enough to wait for the things I really want." Robbie and Bree had recently begun seeing each other, in a very cautious, uncommitted way. He was in love with her and wanted a real relationship, but so far she had shied away from anything more than fooling around.

I watched as Bree's gaze dropped from his, and I also noticed the interested gleam in Thalia's eyes. Weeks ago I had heard gossip that Thalia was hot for Robbie. If Bree's not careful, Thalia will steal Robbie from her, I thought.

Ethan spoke next, with none of his usual joking around. "I'm afraid I'll be weak and lose a really great person in my life." I guessed he was talking about his pot smoking. Around the time he and Sharon had started seeing each other, he'd more or less given up pot, in part because he knew she didn't like it when he smoked.

Sharon, who held Ethan's left hand, looked at him with open affection. "I'm not," she said simply. Then she looked at the rest of us. "I'm terrified of dying," she said.

We kept going around the circle. Jenna was afraid she wouldn't be brave. Raven was afraid of being tied down. Matt was afraid no one would ever understand him. I thought of telling him he should start by trying to understand himself, but I realized this wasn't the right time or place.

"I'm afraid I'll never be able to have what I really want," Bree said in a small voice, looking at the floor.

"I'm afraid of unrequited love," Sky said, her dark eyes as enigmatic as ever.

"I'm afraid of fire," Simon said, and I jerked, startled. My birth parents had burned to death in a barn, and Cal had tried to kill me with fire when I'd refused to join the conspiracy he and his mother were part of. I, too, was afraid of fire.

"I'm afraid of my anger," Alisa said. That surprised me. She looked so sweet.

Then it was my turn. I opened my mouth, intending to say I was afraid of fire, but something stopped me. I felt Hunter's gaze on me, and it was as if he were shining a spotlight on the darkest recesses of my mind, urging me to dredge up my deepest fear.

"I'm afraid I'll never know who I am," I said, and as I said it, I knew it was true.

Hunter was last. In a clear voice he said, "I'm afraid of losing any more people I love."

My heart ached for him. His brother had died at the age

of fifteen, murdered by a dark spirit called a taibhs. And his father and mother had disappeared ten years ago, driven into hiding by the dark wave, a cloud of evil and destruction that had wiped out many covens, including my own birth parents'. He had a younger sister, I knew, and it occurred to me that he must worry about her all the time.

Then I looked at him and found his gaze locked on me, and my skin prickled as if the air were suddenly full of electricity.

A moment later we dropped hands and it was over. I guessed a lot of people would stay to hang out, but I felt oddly antisocial, and I went to snag my coat. The events of the last week had shaken me more than I had admitted to anyone. As of the day before, school was out officially for winter break, and it was a huge relief to finally have hours of free time in front of me so that I could try to begin processing the myriad ways my life had changed in the last three months.

"Robbie?" I said, interrupting his conversation with Bree. They were huddled close, and I thought I heard Robbie cajoling and Bree playfully resisting.

"Oh, hey, Morgan," Robbie said, looking up reluctantly, and then Hunter's voice was at my ear, sending a shiver down my spine as he said, "Can I give you a ride home?"

Seeing the relief on Robbie's face, I nodded and said, "Yeah. Thanks."

Hunter put on his leather jacket and his hat, and I followed him out into the darkness.

2.
Spin

I've been packing up Patrick's things. Last week we had his memorial service—all of Catspaw and some folks from Waterwind were there. I can't believe he's gone. Sometimes I'm sure he's not gone—that he's about to start up the stairs, he's about to call, he'll walk through the door, holding some new book, some new find.

My friend Nancy asked if it had bothered me that he was nearly forty years older than me. It never did. He was a beautiful man, no matter what his age. And even more important, he loved me, he shared his knowledge, he let me learn anything I could. My powers are ten times stronger now than they were when we first met.

Now Patrick's gone. The house is mine, all his things are mine. I'm looking through his books and finding so many I never knew he had. There are books hundreds of years old that I can't even decipher. Books written in code. Spelled books that I can't even open. I'm going to ask Stella for help with these. Since she became Catspaw's leader, I've trusted her more and more.

Without Patrick here to distract me, so many things are becoming clearer. I'm not sure, but I think he worked with dark magick sometimes. I think some of the people who came here worked with darkness. At the time I didn't pay much attention to them. Now I think Patrick often had me spelled so I wouldn't question things. I guess I understand, but I wish he'd trusted me to accept what he was doing and not automatically condemn it.

I managed to open one book, breaking through its privacy charm with a counterspell that took me almost two hours to weave. Inside were things that Patrick never showed me: spells about calling on animals, spells for transporting your energy somewhere, spells to effect change from far away. Not dark magick per se, but proscribed nonetheless; the council says spells to manipulate should never be used lightly. No one in Catspaw would touch a book like this, even though they're Woodbane. But I would. Why shouldn't I learn all there is to know? If the knowledge exists, why should I blind myself to it?

This book is mine now. And I will study it.

—SB

There's something about being with someone in a car at night that makes you feel like you're the only people in the world. I had felt that way three weeks ago, when Cal kidnapped me, spelled me so I couldn't move, and drove me to his house. That night, alone in the car with Cal, it had been unspeakably bad: pure panic, fear, anger, desperation.

I felt differently tonight, with Hunter by my side. Recently, when it became clear that he might have to stay in Widow's Vale for a while, he'd bought a tiny, battered Honda to replace the rental car he'd been driving. The small space inside felt cozy, intimate.

"Thanks for backing us up about joining the two covens," he said, breaking the silence.

"I think it's a good idea. I'd rather know where everyone is and what they're doing."

He gave a short laugh and shook his head. "That's harsh," he said. "I hope someday soon you'll be able to trust other people again."

I tried not to flinch at the thought. I had trusted Cal, and it had almost cost me my life. I had trusted David, and he'd turned out to have a dark side, too. What was it about me that blinded me to evil? Was it my Woodbane blood?

And yet . . . "I trust you," I said honestly, uncomfortable with the feeling of vulnerability those words awoke in me.

Hunter glanced at me, his eyes an unfathomable shade of gray in the darkness. Without speaking he reached across the seat and took my hand. His skin was cool, and my fingers brushed against a callus on his palm. Holding hands with him felt daring, strange. Holding hands with Cal had been so natural, so welcome.

I was seventeen and had had only one boyfriend. I'd known since that remarkable kiss that Hunter and I had a definite connection, but he wasn't my boyfriend, and we'd never been on an official date.

I breathed deeply, willing my pulse to slow down. "I know magick is all about achieving clarity," I said. "But I feel so confused."

"Magick itself is about clarity," Hunter agreed. "But people aren't. Magick is perfect; people are imperfect. When you put the two together, it's bound to get cloudy sometimes. When it's just you and magick, how does it feel?"

I thought back to when I had worked spells, had circles by myself, scryed in fire, used my birth mother's tools. "It feels like heaven," I said quietly. "Like perfection."

"Right," Hunter said, squeezing my hand and turning the steering wheel with the other. His headlights sliced through the night on this winding road toward downtown Widow's Vale. "That's pure magick and only you. But as soon as you add other people into the mix, especially if they aren't totally clear themselves, you get confusion."

"It's not just magick," I said, looking out the window, trying to ignore the exciting feeling of his hand on mine. I didn't know how to put it—despite my two months with Cal, I was still a relative newcomer to the guy-girl thing. I thought that Hunter liked me, and I thought I liked him. But it was so different. Cal had been obvious and persistent in his pursuit of me. What kind of a person was I, liking Hunter, finding him attractive, when until just a few weeks ago I'd thought I was madly in love with Cal? Yet here Hunter was, holding my hand, taking me home, possibly kissing me later. A little shiver went down my spine.

Hunter zoomed around a tight corner, making me lean toward him.

Then he pulled his hand from mine and put it on the steering wheel.

"Whoa," I said, covering my disappointment. "Going a little fast, huh?"

"I can't help it," he said in his crisp English accent. "The brakes don't seem to be working."

"What?" Confused, I glanced over to see his jaw set, his face tense with concentration.

"The brakes aren't working," he repeated, and my eyes widened as I understood the words.

In alarm I looked ahead—we were going downhill, toward the curviest parts of this road, where signs recommended going no more than twenty miles an hour. The speedometer said fifty.

My heart thudded hard, once. "Crap. Downshift?" I said faintly, not wanting to distract him.

"Yes. But I don't want to make us skid. I could turn off the engine."

"You'd lose the steering," I murmured.

"Yes," he said grimly.

Time slowed. The facts—that the road was icy, that we were wearing seat belts, that the car was small and would crumple like a tin can, that my heart was thudding against my ribs, that my blood was like ice water in my veins—all these things registered as Hunter downshifted forcefully, making the engine buck and groan. The whole car shuddered. I

gripped the door handle tightly, my foot pressing a nonexistent brake pedal on the floor. I'm too young to die, I thought.
I don't want to die.

We were in third gear, going about forty miles an hour
downhill. The engine whined, straining uselessly against the
gravity and inertia that pulled the car forward, and we began
to pick up speed again. I glanced at Hunter, hardly breathing.
His face looked bleached in the dim dashboard light, as if he
were carved from bone. I heard the squeal of the wheels and
felt the sickening lurch of the car as we skidded around
another curve, then another.

Hunter downshifted once more, and the whole car
jumped with an annoyed sound. My back hit my seat, and the
car seemed to dance sideways, like a spooked horse. Hunter
grabbed the parking brake and slowly eased it upward. I
didn't feel any effect. Then with a hard jerk Hunter popped
it into place, and the car jolted again and started skidding
sideways, toward a tree-lined ditch. If the car rolled, we
would be crushed. I quit breathing and sat frozen.

He shifted into first gear and simultaneously turned into
the skid so we did an endless, semicontrolled fishtail right in
the middle of Picketts Road. Hunter let us skid, and when we
had slowed enough, he cut the engine. The steering wheel
locked, but it was okay—we were still headed into the spin,
and finally we scraped to a noisy halt at the side of the road,
not six inches from a massive, gnarled sycamore that would
have flattened us if we'd hit it.

After the grinding screeches of the tortured engine and
tires, the silence of the night was broken only by our shallow
panting. I swallowed hard, feeling like my seat belt was the

only thing holding me upright. My eyes felt huge as I searched Hunter's face.

"Are you all right?" he asked, his voice slightly shaky.

I nodded. "You?"

"Yes. That could have been bad."

"You have a knack for understatement," I said weakly. "That *was* bad, and it could have been deadly. What happened to the brakes?"

"Good question," Hunter said. He peered through his window at the dark woods.

I looked around, too. "Oh. We're near Riverdale Road," I said, recognizing this bend in the road. "We're about a mile and a half from my house. This isn't far from where I put Das Boot into a ditch."

Hunter unsnapped his seat belt. "Can we walk to your house?"

"Yeah."

Hunter locked the car where it sat neatly and quietly by the side of the road, as if it hadn't almost killed us. We started walking, and I didn't speak because I could tell Hunter was sending out his senses, and I realized he was searching for other presences nearby. And then it hit me: he wasn't sure the failure of the brakes had been an accident.

Without stopping to think, I flung out my own senses like a net, letting them infiltrate the woods, the night air, the dead grass beneath the snow.

But I felt nothing out of the ordinary. Apparently Hunter didn't, either, because his shoulders relaxed inside his coat, and his stride slowed. He came to a stop and put his hands on my shoulders, looking down at me.

"Are you sure you're all right?" he asked, his voice quiet.

"Yes." I nodded. "It was just scary, that's all." I swallowed. "Do you think that part of the road is spelled? It's so close to where I had my wreck. And Selene—"

"Is nowhere around here. We check every day, and she's gone," said Hunter. Selene Belltower was Cal's mother and the one who'd urged him to pursue me. She'd wanted me and my Woodbane power and my Woodbane coven tools under her control. Failing that, she'd wanted me dead and out of the way. Though she'd fled Widow's Vale weeks ago, I still felt my pulse race whenever I thought of her.

"When you had your wreck, you thought you saw head-lights behind you, right?" Hunter went on. "And you felt magick, didn't you?" He shook his head. "This felt simply mechanical—there just weren't any brakes. I'll call a tow truck from your house, if that's okay."

"Sure," I said, taking a deep breath and trying to unkink muscles still knotted with fear. "And I can give you a ride home."

"Thank you." He hesitated, and I wondered if he was going to kiss me. But he straightened again and took his hands away, and we began walking toward home.

The cold made us walk fast, and at some point Hunter took my hand in his and put them both in his pocket. The feeling of his skin against mine was wonderful, and I wished I could put my arms around him, under his coat. But I still felt unsure of myself with him—there was no way I could be that daring.

As if he'd read my thoughts, Hunter turned and caught

my gaze. I blushed, ducked my head, and walked even faster. I was relieved when we turned onto my street.

My parents and my fourteen-year-old sister, Mary K., were watching a movie in the family room when we got home. Hunter blandly told them he'd had "a little car trouble," and they clucked and fretted while he called the tow service. When he hung up, I looked at the clock—it was a few minutes after eleven.

"Mom, is it okay if I take Hunter to his car and then to his house?" I asked.

Mom and Dad did the usual silent parent-communication thing with each other, then Mom nodded. "I guess so. But please drive extra carefully. I don't know what it is with you and cars, Morgan, but I'm starting to worry about you on the road."

I nodded, feeling a little guilty. My parents didn't know the half of it. Three weeks ago Robbie had saved my life. Unfortunately he had saved it by driving my car through the stone wall of Cal's pool house, where I'd been trapped. My parents (who thought I'd hit a light pole) had lent me some of the money to have the front end repaired.

"Okay," I agreed, and Hunter and I got our coats again and went out to Das Boot, my giant, submarine-like '71 Plymouth Valiant. Automatically I winced as I saw its shiny new front bumper, slate blue hood, and gray-spotted sides. I had to get it painted and soon. This rainbow look was killing me.

Inside my car it was freezing, and its old-fashioned vinyl seats didn't help any. We didn't speak as I drove back to Hunter's car to wait for the tow truck. Hunter seemed lost in thought.

After only a minute Widow's Vale's one tow truck came into view. I'd seen John Mitchell a few weeks before, when I had put Das Boot into the ditch. He flicked a glance at me as he bent to hook up the chain to Hunter's car.

"We lost the brakes," Hunter explained as John began to crank the car onto the bed of the truck.

"Hmmm," John said, and bent beneath the car to take a quick look. When he came up again, he said, "I don't see anything offhand," and spat onto the side of the road. "Besides the fact you don't seem to have any brake fluid."

"Really," said Hunter. His brows rose.

"Yeah," John replied, sounding almost bored. He gave Hunter a clipboard with a paper to sign. "Anyway, I'll bring it to Unser's and he'll fix you up."

"Right," said Hunter, rubbing his chin.

We got back in Das Boot and watched the tow truck take Hunter's car away. I started the engine and headed toward the edge of town, toward the little house he shared with Sky. "No brake fluid," I said. "Can that happen by itself?"

"It can, but it seems unlikely. I had the car tuned up last week, when I bought it," Hunter said. "If there was a leak, the mechanic should have caught it."

I felt a prickle of fear. "So what are you thinking, then?" I asked.

"I'm thinking we need some answers," Hunter said, looking out his window thoughtfully.

Ten minutes later I pulled up in front of his shabby rented house and saw Raven's battered black Peugeot parked out front.

"Are Raven and Sky getting along?" I asked.

"I think so," Hunter answered. "They're spending a lot of time together. I know Sky's a big girl, but I worry about her getting hurt."

I liked seeing this caring side of Hunter, and I turned to face him. "I didn't even know Sky was gay until she and I did our tàth meànma." Weeks ago Sky and I had done what I think of as a Wiccan mind meld. When our thoughts had been joined, I had been surprised to see that she felt such a strong desire for Raven, our resident gothy bad girl.

"I don't know that Sky *is* gay," Hunter said thoughtfully. "She's had relationships with guys before. I think she just likes who she likes, if you know what I mean."

I nodded. I had barely dipped my toes into plain vanilla heterosexual relationships—any variation seemed too mind-boggling to contemplate.

"Anyway," said Hunter, opening his car door and letting in the cold night air, "drive very carefully on your way home. Do you have a cell phone?"

"No."

"Then send me a witch message," he instructed. "If anything the slightest bit out of the ordinary happens, send me a message and I'll come right away. Promise?"

"Okay."

Hunter paused. "Maybe I should borrow Sky's car and follow you home."

I rolled my eyes, refusing to admit I was worried about the lonely drive home. "I'll be fine."

His eyes narrowed. "No, let me get Sky's keys."

"Would you stop? I've driven these roads a million times. I'll call you if I need you, but I'm sure I won't."

He sat back and pulled the door closed. The dome light blinked off.

"You are incredibly stubborn," he remarked conversationally.

I knew he meant well, so I swallowed my tart response. "It's just—I'm very self-reliant," I said self-consciously. "I've always been that way. I don't like owing other people."

He looked at me. "Because you're afraid they'll let you down?"

I shrugged. "Partly, I guess. I don't know." I looked out the window, not enjoying this conversation.

"Look," he said calmly, "I don't know what happened with the car. We don't think Cal and Selene are around, but in fact we don't know where they are or what they're doing. You could be in real danger."

What he said was true, but I felt reluctant to concede the point. "I'll be okay," I said, knowing I was being pointlessly stubborn and unable to stop myself.

Hunter sighed impatiently. "Morgan, I—"

"Look, I'll be fine. Now stop fussing and let me go home." Had I ever been so forthright with Cal? I had wanted so badly for Cal to find me attractive, felt I had fallen so far short of the kind of girl he would want. I had tried to be a more appealing Morgan for him, as stupid and clumsy as my attempts had been. With Hunter, I had never bothered. It felt very freeing to say whatever came to my lips because I wasn't worried about impressing him.

We stared at each other in a standoff. I couldn't help comparing his looks to Cal's. Cal had been golden, exotic, and astoundingly sexy. Hunter was more classical, like a

Greek statue, all shapes and planes. His beauty was cool. Yet as I looked at him, the desire to touch him, to kiss and hold him, grew in me until it was almost overpowering.

He shifted in his seat, and I almost flinched when he brought a cool hand up to stroke my cheek. With that one touch I was mesmerized, and I sat very still.

"I'm sorry," he said, his voice low. "I'm afraid for you. I want you to be safe." He smiled wryly. "I can't apologize for worrying about you."

Slowly he leaned closer, his head blotting out the moonlight streaming through the windshield. Ever so gently his warm lips touched mine, and then we were kissing, kissing hard, and I felt completely exhilarated. When he pulled back, we were both breathing fast. He opened the door again, and I blinked in the glare from the dome light. He shook his head, as if to clear it, and seemed at a loss for words. I licked my lips and looked out the windshield, unable to meet his eyes.

"I'll talk to you tomorrow," he said softly. "Drive carefully."

"Okay," I managed. I watched him walk up to the front porch and wanted to call him back, to throw my arms around him and press against him. He turned then, and I wondered with embarrassment if he had picked up on my feelings. I stepped on the gas and sped off.

With witches, you never know.

3.
Sharing

November 5, 1968

My mind is still reeling from all that I've seen in the past week.

It started when I found Patrick's Turneval Book of Shadows. That's when I discovered that Waterwind was only one of the covens that he'd belonged to. It was the one he had grown up with, back in Seattle, and it was just like Catspaw: Woodbanes who had renounced everything to do with the dark side. But since I started going through his Turneval stuff, I've seen a whole new side of him. What a waste: oh, Patrick, if only you had shared this with me, the way you shared everything else!

I wonder if he thought Turneval would horrify me. How could he not know I'd be open to anything, anything he wanted to show me, teach me, any kind of power? He must have known. Maybe he was biding his time. Maybe he wanted to show me but died too soon.

I'll never know. I only know that I would've loved being in Turneval with him, loved for him to teach me all that it meant to be Woodbane.

On Samhain, instead of going to Catspaw's festivities, I went to a Turneval circle. We started by making circles of power and invoking the Goddess, just like at Catspaw. Then everything changed. The Turneval witches knew spells that opened us to the deepest magick, the magick contained in all the creatures and lives that are no longer part of this earth. For the first time I was aware of a universe of untapped resources, whole strata of energy and power and connection that I had never been taught. It was frightening and unbearably exciting. I'm too much of a novice to use this power, of course—I don't even fully know how to tap into it. But Hendrick Samuels, one of Turneval's elders, gave himself over to it, and he actually shape-shifted in front of us. Goddess, he shape-shifted! Covens talk about shape-shifting like it's the story of Goldilocks—but it's real, it's possible. Before my eyes I saw Hendrick assume the form of a mountain lion, and he was glorious. I have to get close to him so he'll share the secret with me.

This is what Patrick spent his life studying, what he

hid from me. It's what I was meant to do, what I should have been born to but wasn't. I see that now.

—SB

"Your folks don't mind you skipping church?" Bree's dark eyes were dimmed by the ribbon of steam coming from her coffee mug. We were in a coffee emporium in a strip mall off the main road. It was popular on Sunday mornings, and people surrounded us, drinking coffee, eating pastry, reading sections of newspaper.

I made a face and loaded my currant scone with butter. "They mind. Somehow they would be more comfortable about my being Wiccan if I also remained a good Catholic."

"And that's not possible?" Bree asked around a mouthful of bear claw.

I sighed. "It's hard."

Bree nodded, and we ate for a few minutes. I studied her covertly. While she was very familiar to me, still, we were both undeniably different people from who we had been three months ago, when Wicca and Cal came into both our lives. We were feeling our way back to being friends again. Things were still awkward between us sometimes, but it felt good to hang out and talk, anyway.

"I like a lot of things about Catholicism. I like the services and the music and seeing everyone," I said. "Feeling like I belong to something bigger than just my family. But it's hard to wrap my mind around some of it. Wicca just feels so much more natural to me." I shrugged. "Anyway, I just wanted to skip it this week. It doesn't mean that I'm never going back."

Bree nodded again and tugged her black top into place.

As usual, she looked chic and beautiful, perfectly put together, though she was only wearing jeans and a sweater and no makeup. Usually I felt like a lumberjack around her, with my flat chest, strong nose, boring hair, and lame wardrobe. Today I was surprising myself by feeling strong beneath my looks, as if the witch inside might someday be attractive enough for the Morgan outside.

"How's Mary K.?" Bree asked.

I stirred my coffee. "She's been kind of down lately. Since the whole Bakker fiasco, it's like she's walking around waiting for a ton of bricks to fall on her." Bakker Blackburn, my sister's ex-boyfriend, had twice tried to use force to get her to have sex with him.

"That prick," said Bree. "You should put some awful spell on him. Give him Robbie's old acne." In October, in a fit of experimentation, I'd made a magick potion to clear up the terrible acne that had marred Robbie's looks for years. It had had some unexpected side effects, like correcting his bad vision so that he no longer needed his coke-bottle glasses. Without the glasses and the acne, he turned out to be startlingly good-looking.

I laughed. "Now, you know we're not supposed to do things like that."

"Oh, like that would stop you," she said, and I laughed some more. It was true that I had either bent or flat-out broken quite a few of the unwritten Wiccan guidelines for responsible use of magick since I had first discovered my powers. But I was trying to be good.

"Speaking of Robbie," I said leadingly, raising my eyebrows.

Bree looked down at her plate. "Oh, Robbie," she said vaguely.

"Are you going to break his heart?" My voice was light, but we both knew I was serious.

"I hope not," she said, and tapped her finger against her plate. "I don't want to. The thing is—he's just throwing himself at me, heart, soul, and body."

"And the body you want," I guessed.

"The body I'm dying for," she admitted.

"You don't want anything else from him?" I said. "You know Robbie's a really good guy. He'd be a great boyfriend."

Bree groaned and dropped her face onto her hands. "How can you tell? We've known him since we were babies! I know him *too* well. He's like a pal, a brother."

"Except you want to jump him."

"Yeah. I mean, he's gorgeous. He's . . . fabulous. He makes me crazy."

"I don't believe it's only physical," I said. "He wouldn't tie you up in knots if there weren't some emotion going on, too."

"I know, I know," Bree muttered. "I don't know what to do. I've never had this problem before. Usually I know exactly what I want and how to get it."

"Well, good luck," I said, sighing. "So, relationships are heating up all over," I added. "Raven and Sky, Jenna and Simon . . ."

"Yeah," Bree said, cheering up. "Sky and Raven are freaking me out. I mean, Raven's a boyfriend machine."

"Maybe what she was looking for all along was a girl," I said, and we made dorky oh-my-gosh faces at each other.

"Could be. And you think Jenna and Simon?" Bree asked, taking a sip of her coffee.

"I think so. They seem to be interested in each other," I reported. "I hope they do get together. Jenna deserves to be happy after Matt was such an ass to her." I stopped suddenly, remembering that Raven had tried to nail Matt primarily to get him to join her coven—the coven that Bree had also been a member of. The old Kithic.

For a moment Bree looked uncomfortable, as if she too were mulling over the convoluted events of the last month. "Everything changes, all the time," she finally said.

"Uh-huh."

"Anyway," Bree said, "what's with you and Hunter?"

I choked on my coffee and spent the next minute coughing gracelessly while Bree arched her perfect eyebrows at me.

"Uh," I finally said hoarsely. "Uh. I don't know, really."

She looked at me, and I shifted in my seat.

"It just seems that you guys set off sparks when you're together."

"Sometimes," I admitted.

"Do you still love Cal?"

Just hearing his name, especially spoken by Bree, made me wince. Bree had thought she was in love with him. They had slept together before Cal and I started going out, which, as I saw it now, Cal had done partly to drive a wedge between Bree and me so that I'd be all the more dependent on him. I still found it hard to stomach the fact that Cal and Bree had had sex, and he and I hadn't, despite how much I had loved him and thought he loved me.

"He tried to kill me," I said faintly, feeling like the coffee shop was too small.

Compassion crossed her face, and she reached across the table to touch my hand. "I know," she said softly. "But I also know you really loved him. How do you feel about him now?"

I still love him, I thought. I am filled with rage and hatred toward him. He said he loved me, he said I was beautiful, he said he wanted to make love to me. He hurt me more than I can say. I miss him, and I hate myself for being so weak.

"I don't know," I finally said.

As I was opening my car door in the parking lot, out of the corner of my eye I saw a guy come out of the video store next door to the coffee place. I glanced up, and my heart stopped beating. He was looking down at a piece of paper in his hand, but I didn't need to see his face. I'd run my fingers through that raggedly-shorn dark hair. . . . I'd kissed that wide, smooth chest. . . . I'd stared so many times at those long, powerful legs in their faded blue jeans. . . .

Then he looked up, and I saw that it wasn't Cal after all. It was a guy I'd never seen before, with pale blue eyes and bad skin. I stood there, stunned in the bright sunlight, while he gave me a funny look, then walked to his car and got in.

It felt like a full minute before my heartbeat returned to normal. I climbed into Das Boot and drove home. But the whole way, I couldn't help checking my rearview mirror to see if anyone was behind me.

Later that day the phone rang. I raced to answer it, knowing it was Hunter.

"Can I come over?" he asked when I picked up the receiver.

When I'd gotten back from seeing Bree, Mom, Dad, and my sister were already home from church. I felt guilty about not having gone with them, so since then I had been trying to do good-daughter-type stuff around the house— shoveling the front walk, picking up my crap from the living room, unloading the dishwasher. Having Hunter over would kind of wreck my attempts at scoring points with my family.

"Yes," I said quickly. My heart kicked up a beat in response to his voice. "How will you get here?"

Silence. I almost laughed as I realized he hadn't thought about that.

"I'll borrow Sky's car," he said finally.

"Do you want me to come get you?" I asked.

"No. Are your parents there? Can we talk alone?"

"Yes, my parents are here, and we can talk alone if you want to stand out on the front porch with my whole family inside wondering what we're talking about."

He sounded irked. "Why can't we just go to your room?"

What planet did he come from? "I'm sorry, Your Highness, but I don't live by myself," I said. "I'm seventeen, not nineteen, and I live with my parents. And my parents don't think it's a good idea for boys to be in my room, because there's a bed in there!" Then of course the image of Hunter on my bed made my cheeks burn, and I was sorry I had ever opened my big mouth. What was wrong with me?

"Oh, right. Sorry—I forgot," he said. "But I need to speak to you alone. Can you meet me at the little public park that's by that big grocery store on Route Eleven?"

I thought. "Yes. Ten minutes."

He hung up without saying good-bye.

When I got there, Hunter was standing by Sky's car, waiting for me. He opened Das Boot's door and climbed into the front seat. He was in a tense, angry mood, and the funny thing was, I picked up on that just from waves of sensory stuff I got from him, not from the look on his face or his body language. It was as if he was projecting those feelings and I could just sense them. My witch powers were developing every day, and it was wonderful and a bit scary at the same time.

I waited for him to speak, looking out the windshield, catching the faintest hint of his clean, fresh smell.

"I talked to Bob Unser this morning," he said. "There wasn't any brake fluid in the car, but more than that, the actual brake lines had been severed, right by the fluid reservoir."

I turned to stare at him. "Severed?"

He nodded. "Not cut exactly, not as smooth as that. He couldn't say for sure that someone had cut them. But he did say that it was unusual since both brake lines looked fine when he checked the car last week. It didn't seem like they could simply wear through so quickly."

"Did you check the car for spells, magick?" I asked.

"Yes, of course," he said. "There wasn't anything, apart from the spells of protection I'd put on it."

"So what does that mean? Was this an accident, a person, a witch, what?"

"I don't know," he admitted. "I think it was a person

rather than an accident. I think it was a witch because I just don't know that many nonwitches, and I certainly haven't got any nonwitch enemies."

"Could it have been Cal?" I forced myself to ask. "Or Selene?"

"They're the first ones I thought of, of course," he said matter-of-factly, and the hair on my arms rose. I remembered the guy I'd seen in the parking lot this morning—the one I'd thought was Cal.

"But I still don't think they're in the area," he added. "I run a sweep every day, checking this whole area for signs of them, and I haven't picked up on anything. Of course, I'm not as powerful as Selene," he said. "Just because I can't feel her doesn't mean she's truly gone. But I can't help thinking that I would pick up on something if they were still around."

"Like what?" I asked. My mouth felt suddenly dry.

"It's hard to say," Hunter said. "I mean, sometimes I do feel . . . something. But there are so many other things going on that I can't really delineate it." He frowned. "If you were stronger, we could work together, join our powers."

"I know," I said. I was too freaked to bristle at being called weak. "I'm just a newbie. But what about Sky?"

"Well, Sky and I have already joined our powers," he said. "But you have the potential to be stronger than either of us. That's why you must be studying and learning as much as you can. The faster we can get you up to speed, the faster you can help us, help the council. Maybe even join the council."

"Ha," I exclaimed. "There's no way I'm joining the council! Be a hall monitor for Wicca? No thanks!" Then I realized how that must have sounded to Hunter, who was a member of the council himself, and I wanted to take the words back. Too late.

Hunter pressed his lips together and stared out his window. No one else was around: it was a Sunday afternoon and not warm enough for kids to be on the playground. Silence filled my ears, and I sighed.

"I'm sorry," I said. "I didn't mean that. I know that what you do is more important than that. Much too important for me to contemplate doing it," I said honestly. "It's just I can hardly manage to dress myself these days, much less think about doing anything more. Everything is so . . . overwhelming right now."

"I understand," Hunter surprised me by saying. "You've been through a lot. And I know I'm putting a lot of pressure on you, and sometimes I forget how new this is to you. But a talent, a power like yours is rare—maybe once in a generation. I don't want to give you an inflated sense of your own importance, but you should realize that you are and will become an important person in the world of Wicca. There are two ways of dealing with it: You can become a hermit, shutting yourself away from people, studying and learning on your own. Or you can embrace your power and the responsibility it brings and accept the joys and heartbreaks associated with it."

I looked at my lap, feeling self-conscious.

"There's something I wanted to mention to you—a way of acquiring a lot of knowledge quickly. It's called a tàth meànma brach, and it's basically a supercharged tàth meànma."

"I don't understand," I said.

"You do a tàth meànma with a witch who knows a lot more than you, who's more learned and more experienced though not necessarily more powerful," Hunter explained. "The two of you join very deeply and openly and in essence give each other all your knowledge. It would be as if you suddenly had a whole lifetime's worth of learning in a couple of hours."

"It sounds incredible," I said eagerly. "Of course I want to do it."

He gave me a warning look. "It's not something you should decide lightly. It's a big thing, both for you and the other witch. It can be painful and even dangerous. If one witch isn't ready or the two personalities are too dissimilar, the damage can be severe. I heard of one case where one of the witches went blind afterward."

"But I would know so much," I said. "It would be worth the risk."

"Don't decide right now," he went on. "I just wanted to let you know about it. It would increase your ability to protect yourself—the more knowledge you have, the better you'll be able to access your power. And part of the reason I'm telling you this is because you've already attracted the attention of some very powerful people: Selene and the rest of her Woodbane organization. The sooner you can protect yourself, the better."

I nodded. "I wish I knew where they were," I said. "I'm afraid to look over my shoulder. I keep expecting to see Cal or Selene."

"I feel the same way sometimes. Not about them specifically, but I've made enough enemies in my job as a Seeker to have an assortment of witches who would love to see me dead. Which, by the way, is something I've been thinking about in regard to the cut brake line. I'd be stupid if I didn't take every possibility into account." He shifted in his seat. "Really, all I'm trying to say is that we both have to be extra careful from now on. We need to strengthen the protection spells on your car and your house, and my car and house, and Sky's car. We have to be vigilant and prudent. I don't want anything to happen to . . . either of us."

For several minutes we sat quietly, thinking things through. I was worried, but Hunter's presence made me feel safer. Knowing he was in Widow's Vale made me feel protected. How long would I have that feeling? How long before he would have to leave?

"I don't know how much time I'll have here," he said, unnerving me with the accuracy of his response to my thoughts. "It could be another month, or it could be a year or more."

I hated the thought of his leaving and didn't want to examine why. Then his strong hand was brushing back a tendril of hair off my cheek, and my breath caught in my throat. We were alone in my car, and when he leaned closer to me, I could feel the warmth of his breath. I closed my eyes and let my head rest against my seat.

"While I'm here," he said softly, "I'll help and protect you in any way I can. But you need to be strong with or without me. Promise me you'll work toward that."

I nodded slightly, my eyes still closed, thinking, Just kiss me, kiss me.

Then he did, and his lips were warm on mine and I coiled

my hand up to hold his neck. The barest wisp of Cal's image brushed across my consciousness and was gone, and I was drawn into Hunter's light, the pressure of his mouth, his breathing, the hard warmth of his chest as he pressed closer. I felt something else, too—a feathery touch deep inside me, like delicate wings brushing against my very heart. I knew without words, without doubt, that I was feeling Hunter's essence, that our souls were touching. And I thought, Oh, the beauty of Wicca.

4.
Begin

May 2, 1969

My skin is shriveled, and my hair is sticky and stiff with salt. I soaked in the purifying bath for two hours, with handfuls of sea salt and surrounded by crystals and sage candles. But though I can dispel the negative energy from my body, I can't erase the images from my mind.

Last night I saw my first taibhs, and when I think of it, I start shaking. Every Catspaw child hears of them, of course, and we're told scary stories about evil taibhs that steal the souls of Wiccan children who don't listen to their parents and teachers. I never thought they really existed. I guess I thought they were just holdovers from the Dark Ages, along with witches riding brooms, black cats, warts on noses: nothing to do with us today, really.

But Turneval taught me differently last night. I had

dressed so carefully for the rite, wanting to outwitch, out-beauty, outpower every other woman there. They had prom-ised me something special, something I deserved after my months of training and apprenticeship. Something I need-ed to go through before I could join Turneval as a full member.

Now, thinking back, I'm ashamed at how naive I was. I strode in, secure in my beauty, my strength and ruthless-ness, only to find by the end of the evening that I was weak, untaught, and unworthy of Turneval's offering.

What happened wasn't my fault. I was just a witness. The ones leading the rite made mistakes in their limita-tions, in the writing of the spells, the circles of protection— it was the first time Timothy Cornell had called a taibhs, and he called it badly. And it killed him.

A taibhs! I still can't believe it. It was a being and not a being, a spirit and not a spirit: a dark gathering of power and hunger with a human face and hands and the appetite of a demon. I was standing there in the circle, all eager anticipation, and suddenly the room went cold, icy, like the North wind had joined us. Shivering, I looked around and saw the others had their heads bowed, their eyes closed. Then I saw it, taking form in the corner. It was like a miniature tornado, vapor and smoke boiling and coiling in on itself, becoming more solid. It wasn't supposed to do any-thing: we were just calling it for practice. But Timothy had *done it wrong, and the thing turned on him, broke through our circles of protection, and there was nothing any of us could do.*

Death by a taibhs is horrible to watch and sickening to remember. I just want to blank it all out: Tim's screams, the wrenching of his soul from his body. I'm shaking now, just thinking of it. That idiot! He wasn't worthy to wield the power he was offered.

For the first time I understand why my parents, limited and dull as they were, chose to work the gentle kind of magick they did. They couldn't have controlled the dark forces any more than a child can hold back a flood by stuffing a rag in a dike.

Now I'm curled up on my bed, my wet hair flowing down my back like rain, and wondering which way I will choose: the safe, gentle, boring way of my parents or the way of Turneval, with its power and its evil twined together like a cord. Which path holds more terror for me?

—SB

"Open a window. This smell is making me sick," Mary K. complained.

I put down my paint roller and flung open one of my bedroom windows. Instantly frigid air rolled in, dispelling the sour, chemical smell of the wall paint. I stepped back to admire what my sister and I had already done. Two walls of my room were now a pale coffee-with-cream color. The other two walls were still covered by the childish pink stripes I was trying to obliterate. I grinned, already pleased with the transformation. I was changing, and my room was changing to keep up.

"You're only going to live here for another year," Mary K. pointed out, carefully edging a line by the ceiling. A paint-spattered bandanna covered her hair, and though she was in sweatpants and a ratty old sweater, she looked like a fresh-faced teen singer. "Unless you go to Vassar or SUNY New Paltz or something and just commute."

"Well, I don't have to decide about that for a while," I said.

"But why worry about your room now?" Mary K. asked.

"I can't take this pink anymore," I said, rolling a swath of paint over the wallpaper.

"Remember when I asked you if you'd had sex?" Mary K. suddenly said, almost making me drop my roller. "With Cal?"

There it was, the familiar wince and stomach clench I felt whenever that name was mentioned.

"Yeah?" I said warily.

"So, did you guys ever do it? After we talked?"

I took a breath and slowly released it to the count of ten. I focused on rolling a smooth, broad line of paint across the wall, feathering the edges and rolling over any drips. "No," I managed to say calmly. "No, we never did." A bad thought occurred to me. "You and Bakker . . ."

"No," she said. "That was why he always got so mad."

She was only fourteen, though a mature and curvy fourteen. I felt incredibly thankful that Bakker hadn't managed to push her further than she was ready to go.

I, on the other hand, was seventeen. I'd always assumed

that Cal and I would make love someday, when I was ready—but the times he'd tried, I said no. I wasn't sure why, though now I wondered if my subconscious had picked up on the fact that I wasn't in a safe situation, that I couldn't trust Cal the way I would need to trust him to go to bed with him. Yet I had loved the other things we had done: the intense making out, how we had touched each other, the way magick had added a whole other dimension to our closeness. Now I would never know what it felt like to make love with Cal.

"How about Hunter?" Mary K. asked, looking down at me thoughtfully from her ladder.

"What about him?" I tried to sound careless, but I couldn't quite pull it off.

"Do you think you'll go to bed with him?"

"Mary K.," I said, feeling my cheeks heat up. "We're not even *dating*. Sometimes we don't even get along."

"That's the way it always starts," Mary K. said with fourteen-year-old wisdom.

We'd started early, so we finished the walls around lunchtime. While I cleaned up the painting equipment, Mary K. went down to the kitchen and made us some sandwiches. Recently she'd gotten into eating healthy food, so the sandwiches were peanut-butter and banana on seven-grain bread. Surprisingly, they were good.

I polished off my sandwich, then took a sip of Diet Coke. "Ah, that hits the spot," I said.

"All that artificial stuff is bad for you," Mary K. said, but her voice was listless. I regarded her with concern. It really was taking her a while to come out of her depression over Bakker.

"Hey. What are you doing this afternoon?" I asked, thinking maybe we could hit the mall, or go to a matinee movie, or do some other sisterly activity.

"Not much. I thought maybe I'd go to the three o'clock mass," she said.

I laughed, startled. "Church on a Monday? What's going on?" I asked. "You becoming a nun?"

Mary K. smiled slightly. "I just feel . . . you know, with everything going on—I just need extra help. Extra support. I can get that at church. I want to be more in touch with my faith."

I sipped my Diet Coke and couldn't think of anything constructive to say. In the silence I suddenly thought, Hunter, and then the phone rang.

I lunged for it. "Hey, Hunter," I said.

"I want to see you," Hunter said with his usual lack of greeting. "There's an antiques fair half an hour from here. I was wondering if you wanted to go."

Mary K. was looking at me, and I raised my eyebrows at her. "An antiques fair?" was my scintillating reply.

"Yes. It could be interesting. It's nearby, in Kaaterskill."

Mary K. was watching the expressions cross my face, and I pantomimed my jaw dropping. "Hunter, is this a date?" I asked for Mary K.'s benefit, and she sat up straighter, looking intrigued.

Silence. I smiled into the phone. "You know, this sort of sounds like a date," I pressed him. "I mean, are we meeting for business reasons?"

Mary K. started snickering quietly.

"We're two friends getting together," Hunter said, sounding very British. "I don't know why you feel compelled to label it."

"Anyone else coming?"

"Well, no."

"And you're not calling it a date?"

"Would you like to come or not?" he asked stiffly. I bit my lip to keep from laughing.

"I'll come," I said, and hung up. "I think Hunter just asked me out," I told Mary K.

"Wow," she said, grinning.

I skipped upstairs to take a shower, wondering how, when my life was so stressful and scary, I could feel so happy.

Hunter picked me up in Sky's car twenty minutes later. My wet hair hung in a long, heavy braid down my back. I offered him a Diet Coke and he shuddered; then we were on our way to Kaaterskill.

"Why did you care if this was a date or not?" he asked suddenly.

I was startled into an honest reply. "I wanted to know where we stand."

He glanced at me. He was really good-looking, and my brain was suddenly bombarded with images of how he had been when we were kissing, how intense and passionate he'd seemed. I looked out my window.

"And where do we stand?" he asked softly. "Do you want this to be a date?"

Now I was embarrassed. "Oh, I don't know."

Then Hunter took my hand in his and brought it to his mouth and kissed it, and my breathing went shallow.

"I want it to be what you want," he said, driving with one hand and not looking at me.

"I'll let you know when I figure it out," I said shakily.

The antiques fair took place in a huge warehouse-like barn in the middle of rural New York. There weren't many people there—it was the last day. Everything looked kind of picked through, but still, I enjoyed the time with Hunter, the time without magick involved. My mood got even better when I found a little carved box that would be perfect for my mom and an old brass barometer that my dad would love. Two Christmas gifts that I could cross off my list. I was woefully behind on my holiday shopping. Christmas was coming up fast, and I'd barely thought about it. Our coven was planning a Yule celebration, too, but fortunately that didn't involve any gift-giving.

I was engrossed in the contents of an old dentist's cabinet when Hunter called me over. "Look at these," he said, pointing to a selection of Amish-type quilts. I'd always liked Amish quilts, with their bright, solid colors and comforting geometry of design. The one Hunter was pointing to was unusual in that it had a circular motif.

"It's a pentacle," I said softly, touching the cotton with my fingertips. "A circle with a star inside." The background was black, with a nine-patch design in each corner in shades of teal, red, and purple. The large circle touched each of the four sides and was of purple cotton. A red five-pointed star filled the circle, and a nine-patch square was centered in the star. It was gorgeous.

I glanced at the middle-aged woman selling the quilts and cast my senses quickly to see if she was a witch. I picked up nothing. "Is it Wiccan?" I asked so only Hunter could hear.

He shook his head. "More likely just a Pennsylvania Dutch hex design. It's pretty, though."

"Beautiful." Again I ran my fingers gently across the cotton.

The next thing I knew, Hunter had pulled out his wallet and was counting out bills into the woman's hand, and she was smiling and thanking him. She took the small quilt, barely more than four feet square, and wrapped it in tissue before putting it into a brown paper bag.

We headed back to Hunter's car. "That's really beautiful," I said. "I'm glad you bought it. Where will you put it?"

We climbed into his car, and he turned to me and handed me the bag. "It's for you," he said. "I bought it because I wanted you to have it."

The air around us crackled, and I wondered if it was magick or attraction or something else. I took the bag and reached my hand inside to feel the cool folds of the quilt. "Are you sure?" I knew neither he nor Sky had much income—this quilt must have put a huge dent in his budget.

"Yes," he said. "I'm quite sure."

"Thank you," I said softly.

He started the car's engine, and we didn't say anything until he dropped me at my house. I climbed out of the car, feeling uncertain all over again. He got out, too, and coming around to the sidewalk, he kissed me, a soft, quick meeting of the lips. Then he climbed back in Sky's car and drove off before I could say good-bye.

5.
Flicker

May 17, 1970

Spring has finally sprung in Wales. Here in Albertswyth the hills are a new bright green. The women of the village are on their hands and knees, setting plants in their gardens. Clyda and I have been walking over the hills and among the rocks, and she's been teaching me the local herb lore and the properties of the local stone, earth, water, and air. I've been here six months now, on one of life's detours.

Since I found out about Clyda Rockpel from one of Patrick's spelled books, I was determined to find her, to learn from her. It took two weeks of camping on her doorstep, eating bread and cheese, sleeping with my coat pulled over my head before she would speak to me. Now I'm her student, taking knowledge from her like a sea sponge absorbs ocean water.

She's deep, dark, terrifying sometimes, yet the glimmers of her power, the breadth of her learning, her strength and guile in dealing with the dark forces fill me with a giddy exhilaration. I want to know what she knows, have the power to do what she does, have control over what she controls. I want to become her.

—SB

On Tuesday, Mary K. and I once again spent the morning working on my room, touching up messy spots on the walls and painting the woodwork. In the afternoon I persuaded my sister to come shopping with Bree and me. The lure of hanging out with us had outweighed her disapproval of our destination: Practical Magick, an occult store up in Red Kill, ten miles north.

"The good thing about Christmas break," Bree said as she drove through downtown Widow's Vale, "is seeing all the poor saps who have to go to work."

"We're going to be poor working saps one day," I reminded her, watching people weaving in and out of the shops on Main Street. I picked at some speckles of paint on the back of my hand and adjusted the heater vent of Breezy, Bree's BMW.

"Not me," Bree said cheerfully. "I'm going to marry rich and be a lady who lunches."

"Gross!" Mary K. protested from the backseat.

Bree laughed. "Not PC enough for you?"

"Don't you want more than that?" Mary K. asked. "You could do anything you want."

"Well, I was kind of kidding," said Bree, not taking offense. "I mean, I haven't figured out what my life calling is yet. But it wouldn't be the worst thing to be a housewife."

"Bree, please," I said, feeling a shade of our old familiarity. "You would last about two weeks. Then you'd go crazy and become an ax murderer."

She laughed. "Maybe so. Neither of you wants to be a housewife? It's a noble profession, you know."

I snorted. I had no concrete idea what to do with my life—I'd always thought vaguely about doing something with math or science—but I knew now without a doubt that the majority of my life would center on Wicca and my own studies in magick. Everything else was optional.

"No," said my sister. "I never want to get married."

Something in her tone made me crane around from the front seat to look at her. Her face looked drawn, almost haunted, in the gray winter light, and her eyes were sad. I glanced across at Bree and was touched by the instant understanding that passed between us.

"I hear you dumped Bakker in a big way," Bree said, looking at Mary K. in the rearview mirror. "Good for you. He's an ass."

Mary K. didn't say anything.

"You know who's cute in your class?" Bree went on. "That Hales kid. What's his name? Randy?"

"Just plain Rand," said Mary K.

"Yeah, him," said Bree. "He's adorable."

I rolled my eyes. Trust Bree to have scoped out the freshman boys.

Mary K. shrugged, and Bree decided not to press it. Then

she pulled Breezy into a parking spot in front of Practical Magick, and we piled out into the chilly December air.

Mary K. looked at the storefront with only faintly disguised suspicion. Like my parents, she strongly disapproved of my involvement with Wicca, though I'd talked her into coming to a party here recently, and she'd enjoyed it.

"Relax," I said, taking her by the arm and pulling her into the store. "You're not going to have your soul sucked out just by looking at candles."

"What if Father Hotchkiss saw us?" she grumbled, naming our church's priest.

"Then we'd have to ask him what he was doing in a Wicca shop, wouldn't we?" I answered, grinning. Inside, I let go of my sister's arm and took a moment to get my bearings. I hadn't been to Practical Magick since I'd come with Hunter to confront David Redstone, the owner, about using dark magick. It had been profoundly horrible, and being in the store brought back the memories in a wave: Hunter questioning David; David's admission of guilt, wrenched from him against his will.

It hurt to associate those memories with this place, the place I had come to think of as my refuge, a lovely, scent-filled shop full of magickal books, essential oils, crystals, herbs, candles, and the deep, abiding peace of Wicca, permeating everything.

Looking up, I saw Alyce, a gentle sorrow still showing on her face. David had been a dear friend of hers. He had turned over the shop to her, a Brightendale blood witch, when he'd had his power stripped from him. She owned the shop now.

She walked toward me, and we embraced: I was taller than she, and I felt bony and immature next to her womanly roundness. We looked into each other's eyes for a moment, not needing to speak. Then I stepped back to include Bree and Mary K.

"Hi, Alyce," Bree said.

"Nice to see you, Bree," Alyce replied.

"You remember my sister, Mary K.?" I asked.

"Certainly," said Alyce, smiling warmly. "The one who was so taken with The Fianna." The Fianna was a Celtic band that Mary K. and I both loved. Alyce's nephew, Diarmuid, played in it. The only way I'd gotten Mary K. to come to the party here was by luring her with promises of The Fianna playing.

"Yes," said Mary K. shyly.

"We just got in a shipment of really interesting jewelry from a woman who works in Pennsylvania," Alyce said, leading Mary K. over to a glass case. "Come see."

I smiled as Mary K. was drawn to the jewelry. Bree moved down the aisle to examine a collection of altar cloths, and I was free to wander the side of the store that was floor-to-ceiling bookshelves. Soon Alyce joined me.

"How is Starlocket?" I asked. Starlocket was Selene Belltower's old coven. With her disappearance, Alyce had been asked to lead it.

"Going through transitions," Alyce said. "Some people have left, of course—those who'd been drawn to Selene's dark side. The rest of us are trying to heal and move forward. It's very challenging, leading a coven."

"I'm sure you're a wonderful leader," I said.

"Alyce?" I looked up as a man came toward us, holding up a box of black candles. "Do we put out all the stock at once or keep some in the back?" he asked.

"I usually put out as much as the shelves will hold," Alyce said. "Finn, come meet Morgan."

Finn looked like he was in his fifties; tall, and neither thin nor fat, but sturdy looking. He had short, thick hair that was a faded red shot through with white. His eyes were hazel, his skin was fair, and he had faded freckles across his nose and cheeks. I sent out my senses without even deciding to and ran a quick scan. Blood witch. Probably Leapvaughn, I thought. They often had red hair. Then I saw the surprise in his eyes and shut down my senses, vaguely embarrassed, as though I'd been caught in the Wiccan equivalent of seeing someone's underwear.

"Hmmm," Finn said thoughtfully, holding out his large hand. "Pleased to meet you, Morgan." He gave Alyce an odd glance, as if she had introduced him to a questionable character.

Alyce smiled. "Morgan, this is Finn Foster. He's helping me in the shop," she explained. To Finn she added, "Morgan is a dedicated customer." She offered no other explanation, and with Finn's eyes on me I felt even more strongly that I had committed a faux pas.

"Who do you study with?" Finn asked.

"Um, right now a lot by myself, and some with Hunter Niall."

Finn blinked. "The Seeker?"

"Yes."

"You're Morgan Rowlands," Finn said, as if he'd just made a connection.

"Yes." I glanced at Alyce uncertainly, but she just smiled reassuringly.

Finn hesitated, as if debating whether to say something more, but then he just smiled and nodded. "Nice meeting you," he said. "Hope to see you again soon." He gave Alyce a glance and took the box of candles to the other side of the store. A moment later I heard Bree asking him about some clover oil. I looked for Mary K. and saw that she was holding some silver earrings up, looking at them in a small mirror.

"What was that about?" I asked Alyce, and she chuckled softly.

"I'm afraid you're a bit notorious," she said. "I'm sorry if you feel like a performing seal, but lots of people have already heard of your power, your heritage—not to mention what happened with Cal and Selene—and they're curious."

Ugh. I shifted uncomfortably.

Alyce reached past me to straighten some books on a shelf. "Has Hunter talked to you about your studies? About tàth meànma brach?"

"Yes," I answered, surprised by the change of subject.

"What do you think of the idea?" Her clear, blue-violet eyes searched mine.

"It sounded exciting," I said slowly. "I want to do it. What do you think about it?"

"I think it might be a good idea," she said, looking thoughtful. "Hunter's right—you need to learn as much as you can as fast as you can. For almost any other witch I would advise against it. It's hard, and I'm sure Hunter told you it can be dangerous. But you're an exceptional case. Of course, it's your decision alone. But you should consider it carefully."

"Would you do it with me?" I asked.

She looked deeply into my eyes. I had no idea how old she was—in her fifties?—but I saw a wealth of knowledge in her gaze. What she knew could help me, and I suddenly wanted her knowledge with a surprising hunger that I tried not to show.

"I'll think about it, my dear," she said quietly. "I'll talk to Hunter, and we can decide."

"Thank you," I whispered.

"Are you about ready?" Bree called down the aisle. Finn had already rung up her purchases; she held a small green bag with silver handles.

"Yes," I called back. "Where's Mary K.?"

"Right here," my sister said, emerging from the other aisle.

"Did you want those earrings you were looking at?" I asked, and she shook her head, her shiny auburn hair swinging around her shoulders. I wondered if she thought buying those earrings would be like taking witchcraft into the house and resolved to try to put her fears to rest on that point. Maybe I could surprise her with them for Christmas.

It was late afternoon when we headed home in Breezy. I was quiet and full of thought about the possibility of doing the tàth meànma brach with Alyce.

"Why do you like that store so much?" Mary K. asked from the backseat.

"Don't you think it's cool?" Bree asked. "Even if I wasn't into Wicca, I would still be into the candles and jewelry and incense and stuff."

"I guess." My sister sounded subdued, and I knew she

was struggling with the conflict of liking anything that had to do with witchcraft while remaining true to her own religion and to my parents. She looked out her window, distant and withdrawn. None of us spoke for several miles, and I looked out my window at the rapidly darkening landscape, the rolling hills, the old farms, the snow clinging to everything. With a start I realized that Bree had taken her old route toward home and that we were in Cal's neighborhood. My heart sped up as we drew closer to the large stone house he had shared with his mother. I hadn't been past here since the night I'd almost died in the pool house, and my skin broke out in a clammy sweat at the memory.

"I'm sorry," Bree murmured as she realized where we were.

I swallowed and didn't say anything, my hand clenching the door handle tightly, my breathing fast and shallow. Relax, I told myself. Relax. They're gone. They're nowhere around. Hunter looks for them—scries for them every day—and he hasn't found them. They're gone. They won't hurt you.

As we passed, my eyes were irresistibly drawn to the house. It looked dark, abandoned, forbidding. I recalled the first floor, with its large kitchen, the huge living room with a fireplace where Cal and I had kissed on the sofa. Selene's hidden, spelled private library that I had found, where I had discovered Maeve's Book of Shadows. Cal's room that ran the length of the attic. His wide, low bed where we had kissed and touched each other. The pool house, where he had trapped me and tried to burn me to death . . .

I felt like I was choking and swallowed again, unable to move my eyes away. Then I stared hard as a flickering light, as if from a candle, passed in front of a dark window. Just one moment and it was gone, but I was sure I had seen it. Wildly I looked over at Bree for her reaction, but her eyes were on the road, her hands poised on the leather steering wheel. In the backseat Mary K. gazed out her window, unhappiness making her face seem younger, rounder.

"Did you—" I started to ask. I stopped. Was I sure I had seen it? I thought so. But what was the point of mentioning it? Mary K. would be upset and worried. Bree wouldn't know what to do, either. If only Hunter was here, I thought, and then grimaced as I realized what would be set in action if Hunter had seen it: a full-blown investigation, worry, trouble, fear.

And had I really seen it? A flickering candle in an abandoned house, at night, for just a moment? I leaned my head against the cold car window, my heart aching. Was this ordeal never going to be over? Would I ever relax again?

"Did we what?" Bree asked, glancing at me.

"Nothing," I mumbled. Surely it had been my imagination. Cal and Selene were gone. "Never mind."

6.
The Lueg

March 18, 1971

At the age of twenty-seven, I have completed the Great
Trial. It was four days ago, and I am only now able to hold
a pen and sit up to write. Clyda thought I was ready, and
I was so eager to do it that I didn't listen to the people who
warned me not to.

The Great Trial. I have wondered how to describe it,
and when my words get close, I want to cry. Twenty-seven is
young—many people are never ready. Most people, when
they do it, are older, have been preparing for years. But I
insisted I was ready, and in the end Clyda agreed.

It took place on top of Windy Tor, past the Old Stones
left by the Druids. Below me I could hear the waves crashing against rocks in a timeless rhythm. There was no moon,
and it was as black as the end of the world. With me were

Clyda and another Welsh witch, Scott Mattox. I was naked, sky clad, and we cast the circle and started the rite. At midnight Clyda held out the goblet. I stared at it, knowing I was scared. It was the Wine of Shadows: where she had gotten it, I don't know. If I passed the Great Trial, I would live. If I didn't pass, this wine would kill me. I took the goblet with a shaking hand and drank it.

Clyda and Scott sat nearby, staying to keep me from going over the edge of the cliff. I sat down, my lips numb, muttering all the spells of power and strength that I knew. Then the first needlelike tingles of pain started in my fingertips, and I cried out.

It was a long, long night.

And here I am, alive, on the other side. I am wasted by fasting, by vomiting, by a sharp-edged sickness in my gut that makes me wonder if they fed me glass. This morning I saw myself in the mirror and screamed at the dull-haired, hollow-eyed, greatly aged woman I beheld. Clyda says not to worry: my beauty will come back with my strength. What is it to her? She was never beautiful and has no idea how it feels to lose it.

Yet hollowed out as I am, like a tree struck by lightning, I can tell the difference. I was strong before, but now I'm a force of nature. I feel like wind, like rain, like lava in my strength. I'm in tune with the universe, my heart beating to its primordial, deeply held thrum. I'm made of *magick, I'm walking magick, and I can cause death or life with a snap of my fingers.*

Was the Great Trial worth this? The illness, the screaming agony, the clawed, ripped hands, the gouges in my thighs made when I was shrieking in terror and desperation and trying to feel anything normal, anything recognizable, even physical pain? My brain was split open and put on display, my body was turned inside out. Yet in the destruction is the resurrection, in the agony is the joy, in the terror is the hope. And now I've taken that terrible, mortal journey and I've come through it. And I'll be like a Goddess myself, and lesser beings will follow me. And I'll found a dynasty of witches that will amaze the world.

—SB

"So if your mother comes home, what should I do?" Hunter asked. "I mean, is she going to hit me with a cooking pan?"

I grinned. "Only if she's in a bad mood." It was Wednesday, my parents were at work, Mary K. was upstairs, and we were getting ready to study. "Anyway, I told you I could come to your place," I reminded him.

"Sky and Raven are at my place," he said. "I assume they wanted privacy."

"Really?" I asked with interest. "Are they getting serious?"

"I didn't come here to gossip," he said primly, and I wanted to smack him. I was trying to think of a clever reply when he looked around the kitchen restlessly.

"Let's go up to your room," he said, and I blinked.

"Uh," I began. Boys were *so* not allowed upstairs in our house.

"You said you'd made an altar," he said. "I want to see it. Your room is where you do most of your magick, right?" He stood up, pushing his hand through his pale hair, and I tried to gather my thoughts.

"Um." The only time Cal had ever been in my room was just for a minute, after Bree had almost broken my nose during a volleyball game at school. Even then my mom had gotten twitchy, despite the fact that I was a total invalid and hardly feeling romantic.

"Come on, Morgan," he coaxed. "We're working. I'll try not to jump you, if that's what you're afraid of."

My face burned with embarrassment, and I wondered what he would do to me if I zapped him with witch fire. I was almost willing to find out.

"Sorry," he said. "Let's start over. Please, may I see the altar you made in your room? If your parents come home unexpectedly, I'll do a quick look-over-there spell and get the hell out of here, okay? I don't want to get you in trouble."

"It's just that it's my parents' house," I said stiffly, standing up and leading the way toward the foyer. "I try to respect their rules when I can. But let's go up quickly. I want you to see it." I plodded up the stairs, intensely aware of his quiet tread behind me.

I was thankful that my room was no longer pink and stripy. Sea grass window shades replaced my frilly curtains, complementing my new café-au-lait-colored walls. The old cream-colored carpet had been pulled up, and I had a simple jute area rug instead. I loved my new room but stood nervously by my desk as Hunter looked around, taking it all in. I went to the closet and pulled out the old camp footlocker that served as my altar, complete with violet linen cloth, candles, and four special objects that represented the four elements.

My single bed seemed to take on mythic proportions, almost filling the room, and I blushed furiously, trying to wipe the image of Hunter + bed out of my mind.

He looked at my altar.

"It's pretty basic," I muttered. "It's hard because I have to keep it hidden."

He nodded, then glanced up at me. "It's fine. Nice. Perfectly appropriate. I'm glad you made one." His voice was calm, reassuring. I pushed the altar back in my closet and artfully draped my bathrobe to cover it. Should we go back downstairs? I wondered, but as I came out of my closet, I saw that Hunter was sitting casually on my bed, his fingers playing with the smooth texture of my down comforter. With no warning I wanted to throw myself on him, press him down against the mattress, kiss him, be physically aggressive in a way I never had with Cal. And then of course as soon as that thought crossed my brain, I recoiled, knowing with certainty how attuned Hunter was to my every feeling. Oh, man.

But his face remained neutral, and he said, "Have you been memorizing the true names of things?"

"Sort of," I said, feeling guilty. I hadn't done much studying since the David incident, but before that I'd made a start on my memorization. I pulled out my desk chair and sat down in it, and at that moment Mary K. tapped lightly on the door and came in, not waiting for me to invite her. She stopped dead when she saw Hunter sitting on my bed, her mouth open in an almost comical O. She looked from him to me and back again, and even Hunter grinned at her expression, his normally serious face lighting up, making him look younger and lighthearted.

"We have to get a lock for that door," he said cheerfully, and I wanted to die. My sister's eyebrows rose, and she looked fascinated.

"I'm sorry," Mary K. said. "I just wanted to ask you about dinner—but I'll come back later."

"No, wait," I started to say, but she had already whirled out the door, closing it behind her with an audible click. I glanced back at Hunter to see him grinning again.

"I feel like a fox in a henhouse full of Catholic girls," he said, looking pleased. "This is doing wonders for my ego."

"Oh, like your ego needs help," I retorted, then wanted to bite my tongue.

But Hunter didn't take offense and instead said, "What names have you been studying?"

Huge, long freaking lists, I wanted to say. I took a deep breath and said, "Um, wildflowers and herbs of this geographic zone, ones that bloom in spring, summer, and fall and are dormant in winter. Ones that are poisonous. Plants that can counteract spells, either good or bad. Plants that neutralize energy." I named ten or eleven of them, starting with maroc dath—mayapple—then paused, hoping he was suitably impressed. Learning just the English or Latin names of hundreds of different plants would have been quite a feat, but I had also learned their true names, their magickal names, by which I could use them in spells, find them, increase or decrease their properties.

Hunter, however, looked underwhelmed. His green eyes were impassive. "And under what condition would you use maroc dath in a spell?"

I hesitated, something about his voice making me think carefully about his question. Maroc dath, maroc dath—I knew it as mayapple, a wild plant with a white flower that bloomed before the last frost of the year . . . used to clarify potions, to make a healing ointment, to . . .

Then I got it. Maroc dath wasn't mayapple. "I meant maroc *dant,*" I said with dignity. "Maroc dant. Mayapple." I tried to remember if maroc dath was something.

"So you're not studying spells in which you use menstrual blood," Hunter said, his eyes on mine. "Maroc dath. Menstrual blood, usually that of a virgin. Used primarily in dark rites, occasionally in fertility spells. That's not what you meant?"

Okay, now I wanted the earth to swallow me. I closed my eyes. "No," I said faintly. "That's not what I meant."

When I opened my eyes again, he was shaking his head. "What would happen if you did that in a spell?" he asked rhetorically. "What happens if you don't know all of this and therefore make errors in your spells?"

My first instinct was to throw a pillow at him. Then I remembered that he was trying to get me to learn so I would be protected. He was trying to help me. I remembered that I had told him I trusted him, and that it had been true.

With my next breath an awareness came over me, something unconnected to what Hunter and I were talking about, and my eyes widened and flew to his face.

"Do you feel it?" I whispered, and he nodded slightly, his whole body tense and still. I moved cautiously toward him, and he reached out his hand to clasp mine. Someone was scrying for me, someone was trying to find me. I sat next to Hunter on the bed, barely conscious of the warmth of his thigh against mine. As one, we closed our eyes and sent out our senses, dissolving the barriers between us and the world, reaching out toward our unseen spy as he or she reached out toward us.

I began to get a sense of a person, a person shape, an energy pattern—and in the next instant it was gone, snuffed as quickly as a candle, without even a wisp trail of smoke to lead me to it. I opened my eyes.

"Interesting," Hunter muttered. "Did you get an identity?"

I shook my head and untangled my fingers from his. He looked down at our hands as if he hadn't known they were joined.

"I have something to tell you," I said, and then I gave him the story of possibly seeing a candle in a window at Cal's house the day before.

"Why didn't you tell me immediately?" he asked, looking angry.

"It just happened last night," I began, defending myself. Then I stopped. He was right, of course. "I—I didn't know what to do," I offered awkwardly. "I figured I was making a big deal out of nothing, just being paranoid." I stood up, moved away from the bed, and pushed my hair over my shoulder.

"Morgan of course you should have told me," Hunter said. His jaw tensed. "Unless you have a good reason not to."

What was he trying to say? "Yes," I said sarcastically. "That's it. I'm in league with Cal and Selene, and I didn't want to tell you because when I *give* myself to the dark side, I *won't* want you to know about it."

Hunter looked like I had slapped him, and he stood quickly, so we were only inches apart and he was towering over me, bright spots of anger appearing on his fair cheeks. His hands gripped my shoulders, and my eyes widened. I jerked away from him, slapping his hands away, and we stared at each other.

"Don't ever joke about that again," he said in a low voice. "That isn't funny. How can you even say something like that after what you saw David Redstone go through?"

I gasped, remembering, and to my horror, hot tears welled in my eyes. It *had* been stupid and appalling to throw that at Hunter after seeing it in reality. What had I been thinking?

Deliberately Hunter stepped back, away from me, and pushed his hand through his hair. A muscle in his jaw twitched, and I knew he was trying hard to control himself.

"I never lose my temper," he muttered, not looking at me. "My whole job, my whole life is about being calm and objective and rational." Then he glanced up, and his eyes were like green water, cool and clear and beautiful, and I felt caught by them, the fire of my anger doused. "What is it about you that gets under my skin? Why do you get to me?" He shook his head.

"We just rub each other the wrong way sometimes," I said clumsily, sinking back down into my desk chair.

"Is that what you think it is?" he asked cryptically. He sat down on my bed again, and I had no idea how to answer him. "All right," he said, "back to the candle. I believe that you saw something. Selene's house has been spelled inside and out with ward-evil, confusion, barrier spells, you name it. A member of the council and I worked for hours after the fire, trying to seal the house and dispel the negative energy from it. Obviously we didn't do enough."

"Do you think it's Cal, or Selene, back inside?" I asked. Had that been Cal I saw in the window, Cal, so close?

"I don't know. I can't see how they could get in, after everything we did. But I can't dismiss the possibility. I'll have to check into it."

Of course he would. He was a Seeker. I realized then that I hadn't wanted to tell him in case it *had* been Cal I'd seen. Even after all that Cal had done, I didn't want Hunter to be seeking him. A vision of David Redstone, weeping and writhing as his power left him, rose up in my mind. I couldn't bear the thought of Cal suffering the same torment.

Hunter's face was serious and still. "Look," he said, standing up and reaching into his backpack. "Let's scry together, right now, joining our energy. Let's just see what happens." He took a purple silk bundle out of the backpack and unwrapped it. Inside was a large, dark, flattish stone. "This was my father's lueg," he said, his voice expressionless. "Have you scryed with a stone before?"

I shook my head. "Only with fire."

"Stones are as reliable as fire," he told me, sitting cross-legged on the floor. "Fire is harder to work with but offers more information. Come sit down."

I sat across from him, our knees touching, as if we were

about to do tàth meànma. Leaning forward, I looked into the flat, polished face of the stone, feeling the familiar excitement of exploring something new in Wicca. My hair draped forward, brushing the stone. Quickly I gathered it at the base of my neck and with practiced gestures twisted it into a braid. I didn't bother securing the end but let it hang behind me.

"It seems like not too many girls have long hair anymore," Hunter said absently. "They all have short, layery . . ." He motioned with his hands, unable to come up with the vocabulary to describe modern do's.

"I know," I said. "I think about cutting it sometimes. But I hate fussing with a style. This way I never have to think about it."

"It's beautiful," Hunter said. "Don't cut it." Then he blinked and became businesslike, while I once again tried to get my bearings on the peaks and valleys of our interaction. "Right. Now, this is just the same as scrying with fire. You open yourself to the world, accept what knowledge the universe offers you, and try to not think: just be. Just like with fire."

"Got it," I said, still processing the fact that Hunter liked my hair.

"Good. Now, we're looking for Cal or Selene," Hunter said, his voice softening and fading.

We leaned toward each other, our heads almost touching, our hands joined lightly on the lueg. It was like looking into a black pool in a woods, I thought. Like looking down a well. As my breathing shifted and slowed and my consciousness expanded gently into the space around me, the lueg began to seem like a hole in the universe, an opening into incomprehensible wonders, answers, possibilities.

I could no longer feel anything physically: I was suspended in time, in space, and only existed because of my thoughts and my energy. I felt Hunter's life force near mine, felt his warmth, his presence, his intelligence, and nothing startled me. Everything was fine.

In the face of the stone I began to see swirls of gray mist, like striated clouds, and I released any expectations I'd had and simply watched to see what they would become. Then it was like watching a video or a moving photograph: I saw a person, walking toward me, as if looking into a camera. It was a middle-aged man, a handsome man, and he looked both surprised and alarmed and intensely curious. I'd seen him before, but I couldn't think where.

"Goddess," Hunter muttered, his breath suddenly coming sharp and fast. I felt my consciousness flare.

"Gìomanach," said the man softly. His face was lined, his hair gray, his eyes brown. But there was something of Hunter in the shape of his jaw, the angle of his cheek.

"Dad," Hunter said, sounding strangled.

I gasped. Hunter hadn't seen either of his parents in ten years, and though we'd talked about the possibility of his trying to find them, as far as I knew, he'd done nothing about it yet. What was happening?

"Gìomanach," said the man again. "You're grown. My son . . ." He looked away. In the background I could barely make out a house, painted white. I heard a seagull cry faintly and wondered where Hunter's father had been all this time, where he was now.

"Dad," Hunter said. I felt the coiled tension of his emotions; it almost caused me pain. "Linden—"

"I know," said the man, looking older and sadder. "I know. Beck told us how your brother died. It wasn't your fault. It was his own fate. Listen, my son—your mother—"

Then the picture changed as a dark presence washed across the face of the lueg. It was like a cloud, a purple-black vapor roiling across the lueg, and Hunter and I watched unspeaking as the dark wave focused and concentrated, blotting out his father's face, the whitewashed window.

With a jolt Hunter snapped back, straightening, his eyes flicking open to stare widely at me, and I gazed at him, seeing his pale face as the grounding of my reality.

My temples were damp with sweat, and my hands were shaking. I rubbed my palms against my corduroys and tried to swallow but couldn't. I knew I had just seen the dark wave in the stone—the dark wave that had consumed my ancestors and almost every member of my ancestral coven almost twenty years before. The dark wave that we believed was somehow connected to Selene.

Hunter spoke first. "Do you think the dark wave took my father just then?" he asked, his voice hoarse.

"No!" I said strongly. He looked so lost. Without thinking I rose to my knees and clasped him in my arms, cradling his head against my chest. "I'm almost sure it didn't. It was more like it passed in front of the stone. Between us and him. I can't believe it, Hunter, that was your father. He's alive!"

"Yes," Hunter said. "I believe he is." He paused, then said. "I wonder what he was trying to tell me about Mum."

I was silent, unable to think of anything comforting to tell him.

"I've got to tell the council," he mumbled against my shirt.

After a few moments he pulled back slightly, and reached up to brush my damp hair away from my face. I looked in his eyes and couldn't read the emotions there. Cal's emotions had always seemed so transparent: desire, admiration, light-hearted flirtation. Hunter was still mostly unreadable to me.

Then I thought, To hell with it, and before either of us realized it, I bent down, put my hands on his shoulders, and pressed my lips against his, keeping my eyes open. I saw the flash of surprise, the sudden ignition of desire, and then his eyes drifted closed and he pulled me backward with him to the floor. I was on top of him, his chest against mine, our legs tangled together.

I don't know how long we lay against the hard floor, the unforgiving jute rug, kissing again and again, but finally I heard a furtive tap on my door and Mary K.'s quiet voice: "Mom just pulled up."

Flushed, breathing hard, I trotted downstairs and helped Mom unload groceries from her car, and ten minutes later when I went back to my room, Hunter was gone, and I had no idea how he had managed to leave without any of us noticing.

7.
Circle of Three

November 8, 1973

Clyda fainted again yesterday. I found her at the bottom of the stairs. This is the third time in two weeks. Neither of us have mentioned it, but the fact is that she is old. She hasn't taken care of herself, she's worked too much magick with too few limitations, and she's dabbled too freely with the dark forces.

That's a mistake I never make. Yes, I'm part of Turneval, and yes, I call on the dark side. But never without protecting myself. Never without precautions. I don't drink from that cauldron without making sure it will be refilled.

At any rate, Clyda's health is Clyda's concern. She doesn't ask for or want my care, and now I need her less and less in my studies. Since the Great Trial, I can learn *anything easily; of course, the strength and the weakness of Wicca is that there's always more to be learned.*

I just reread this entry and can't believe I'm yapping on about an old woman's health when just last night my life changed again. Clyda finally introduced me to some members of her coven, Amyranth. Even now my skin gets chilled, just writing the name. I won't lie: they terrify me, by reputation, by their very existence. And yet I'm so drawn to them and their mission. I have no doubt I was meant to be part of them. From birth I was marked to be in Amyranth, and to deny that would be lying to myself. Oh, I have to go—Clyda is calling.

—SB

There were only four other cars in the parking lot of St. Mary's when I pulled in to drop off Mary K. Probably thirty years ago, weekday-morning services were more attended, but nowadays it seemed amazing that Father Hotchkiss bothered to have them at all.

"You sure you want to go?" I asked Mary K. "Wouldn't you rather just go get coffee instead?"

My sister shook her head but made no move to get out of the car.

"What's going on, Mary K.?" I asked. "You seem so unhappy lately. Is it because of Bakker?"

Again she shook her head, looking out her window. "Not just Bakker," she said finally. "All guys. I mean, look at you and Cal. And Bree and all her boy toys. Guys are just . . ."

"Losers?" I suggested. "Jerks? Imbeciles?"

She didn't smile. "I just don't get it," she said. "It's just—I feel like I never want to date again. Never want to be vulnerable again. And I hate that. I don't want to go through my whole life alone."

I closed my mouth hard before I could say something stupid like, You're only fourteen, don't worry about it.

Instead I said, "I know how you feel."

She looked at me, troubled, and I nodded.

"I feel the same way sometimes. I mean, Cal was my first boyfriend, and look what a mistake that turned out to be. After that, how can I ever be sure of any guy again?"

"You can be sure of Hunter," she said. "He's a good guy."

"I think so. But then I think, Cal seemed like a good guy, too." I grimaced. "You know what the really sick thing is?"

"What?"

"I miss Cal," I admitted. "I felt like I knew him, like I understood him. Now I know he was lying to me, using me, setting me up. But it didn't feel that way at the time, so I don't remember it that way. I'm drawn to Hunter, really drawn to him, but I feel like I don't know him and never will."

We sat in Das Boot, feeling depressed. Instead of cheering her up, I had only brought myself down. "I'm sorry," I said. "I didn't mean to go off on my own problems."

"Want to come to church with me?" Mary K. asked with a touch of humor.

"No." I gave a tiny laugh. "Want to come to Practical Magick with me?"

"No. Well, I'd better go in. I'll walk home after. Thanks for the ride."

"Sure."

"And thanks for talking, too." She gave me a sweet smile. "You're a good sister."

"You are, too," I said. I loved her so much. She got out and walked up the church steps, and I put Das Boot in gear and headed north, to Red Kill and Practical Magick.

I'd come to Practical Magick looking for Christmas gifts, but once I got there, I realized I really wasn't in the mood to shop. I've got time, I told myself. I'd get those silver earrings for Mary K., and then everyone in my immediate family would be accounted for. That left my aunt Eileen and her girlfriend Paula, my aunt Maureen and her husband and kids, and Robbie . . . and after that I was in a gray area. Should I give Hunter a gift? It seemed almost too intimate for whatever our relationship was—but on the other hand, he'd bought me my beautiful hex quilt. And then what about Bree? Were we exchanging gifts this year or not? I sighed. Why did it all have to be so confusing?

A comforting voice interrupted my thoughts. "You look like you need to take your mind off your troubles. Come up and see my new apartment," Alyce suggested. After David's departure, she'd moved into one of the apartments upstairs from the store; it had been David's aunt Rosaline's apartment. David had inherited the shop—and Rosaline's considerable debts—when she'd died not long ago. Trying to find a way out of the debts was what had led him into his disastrous experiment with dark magick. Now that Alyce owned Practical Magick, she was paying back the money Rosaline had owed, on a long-term schedule.

Alyce told Finn where we'd be, and then we went out the front doors. "Since I'm running the shop, it makes sense to live close by, and it saves on rent," Alyce explained. Outside were three other doors, all in a line to the right of the store's glass double entrance. Alyce unlocked the door in the middle, and we went up a steep, narrow wooden staircase.

At the top of the stairs were two small, narrow apartments. Alyce led me through the door on the left. The living room was small and bare but freshly painted a warm cream color. Sitting on a surprisingly modern couch was Sky Eventide, reading a leather-bound book.

"Hey," I said. I hadn't seen her since last Saturday's circle.

"Hi," she answered, searching my face. I wondered if Hunter had told her about our vision of his father and about the dark wave.

"Sky and I have been working together," Alyce explained, stepping into the tiny windowless kitchen to make tea. I sat down on a large pillow on the floor.

"When you came in today, I thought maybe the three of us could have a circle," Alyce went on, getting out cups and saucers. "It'll help center you, Morgan. Also, you and Sky are both working with unanswered questions, and it could be helpful."

I thought about the two circles I had been to recently where my powers had been nonexistent and dreaded the idea of feeling that again.

"Yeah, okay," I said, taking the cup of tea that Alyce offered me.

Our circle was small, just the three of us, and somehow intensely *Alyce*: open, receptive, nurturing, strong, very womanly.

We stood, hands linked, in the middle of the living room. Pale winter sun streamed through the windows. Closing our eyes, we each chanted our personal power calls.

"An di allaigh, ne ullah," I began.

Sky and Alyce each quietly chanted to themselves: Alyce's was in English, while Sky's sounded more like mine, Celtic, old, incomprehensible. Three times we walked deasil around our central candle. By the third cycle I felt power flowing from Sky's fingers to mine, from my fingers to Alyce's. The power had a distinct and different quality: eternal, life enhancing.

Then Alyce invoked the four elements, the Goddess and the God, and said, "Lady and Lord, we are each on a personal quest. Please help us to be open to the answers that the universe provides. Please help us open our minds to the world's wisdom.

"My quest is as leader of Starlocket," Alyce went on. "Help me open my consciousness to receive the wisdom I need to guide the women and men of my coven. Help me understand why I have been chosen as leader. Help me fulfill my duties with love."

Then her blue-violet eyes were on Sky, and she nodded. Sky looked thoughtful, then said, "My quest is . . . whether I'll live up to my parents' heritage. Whether my magick will be as strong, as pure as theirs."

I looked at her, surprised to hear her doubt her own power and ability. She'd always struck me as arrogant, even overconfident, and I knew she had much more knowledge and spellcraft than I did. Now I saw that she had weaknesses, too.

Alyce looked at me, and I felt unprepared. This wasn't what I had come here for, and I had no ready statement. Which quest should I mention? I had so many unanswered questions: about Cal, Selene, Maeve's tools, my natural father, Hunter, Bree. . . . Where to begin?

"No, dear," Alyce said softly. "It's more than that."

Oh. Then I thought of the circle we'd had at Sharon's house, and it came to me. "My personal quest is about my own nature," I said, knowing it was true as the words left my mouth. "Am I more likely to lean toward evil because of my Woodbane blood? Will I have to fight it twice as hard as anyone else? How can I learn to recognize evil when I see it? Am I . . . can I escape the darkness?"

I felt rather than saw Alyce's approval that I had found the right questions, and Sky's piqued interest and slight alarm. We held hands for a moment longer, just standing there, and I felt the power flowing among the three of us, almost like an electric current. I am strong, I thought. And I have good friends. Hunter, Robbie, Bree, Alyce, even Sky— they would all stand by me and help me to make the right choices. For a moment I held that sure knowledge in my mind, and it gave me a sense of comfort and peace.

Then we walked widdershins three times, Alyce disbanded our circle, and we snuffed the candle.

"Thank you both," Alyce said. She began to put away her ritual cups. "Now my apartment will be blessed with good energy. And we've each found a question in our hearts that must be answered before we move forward."

"How do we find the answer?" Sky asked, sounding frustrated.

Alyce laughed and said gently, "That's part of the question, I'm afraid."

We stayed in Alyce's apartment for another half hour or so, just talking, enjoying one another's company. Then Alyce had to go back to the shop, so Sky and I reluctantly left. "That was nice," Sky said as we came out onto the street.

"Yeah." I smiled, enjoying the moment of uncomplicated friendliness.

"Well, see you later." She walked down the street to where her car was parked.

As I started Das Boot, I thought about our circle. Oddly, I felt more afraid than I had before, now that I had openly acknowledged my greatest fear. I kept glancing over my shoulder the whole way home, as if expecting the dark wave to loom up in my rearview mirror.

Not really thinking, I started to take the road home that led past Cal's old house. At the last minute I realized what I was doing and swerved back into my lane, causing an angry honk from in back of me. I made an I'm-sorry kind of wave and took another route home. I didn't want to pass his house. Not today.

8.
Attacked

Samhain, 1975

Last night my two-year apprenticeship with Amyranth ended. So much has changed in my life in the past five years. When I think back to who and what I was, it's like looking back at a different lifetime, a different person. Who I am now is so much more intense and fulfilling.

We're in northern Scotland now, and it's as bleak and forbidding a place as there is. The land is wild here, and I love it, even though I know I wasn't meant to live here. But here we are, and my bones are soaking up the power that seeps from the very rocks in this place.

Two years ago, when I was inducted into Amyranth, I'd heard only vague rumors of dark waves. Since then there have been three events that I know of, but I wasn't allowed to participate in them or know the details. Last night that changed.

The coven we took was Wyndenkell, and it was older than anyone knew. It had existed for at least 450 years. I can't imagine that. In America, most of our covens have existed for less than a hundred. The magick here is ancient and compelling, which is why we wanted it.

I'm bound not to describe the event, nor what we did to call the wave. But I will say that it was the most terrifying, exhilarating event I've ever witnessed. The sight of the huge, fierce wave, the purplish black color of a bruise, sweeping over the gathered circle—feeling its icy wind snatching the souls and power of the witches, feeling its energy being fused into me, like lightning—well, I'm a changed woman, a changed witch. I'm a daughter of Amyranth, and that fact alone gives my life meaning and joy.

Now the Wyndenkell coven's knowledge and magick are ours. As they should be.

—SB

"Now, this is a nice car," Hunter said, running his hand over Breezy's leather seats. "German engineering, fuel efficient."

My eyes narrowed. Was that a dig against Das Boot? It wasn't my car's fault that it was made before fuel economy became a desired trait. I tried to glare at Hunter, but I couldn't hold a grudge. It was just too beautiful a Friday, sunny, perfectly clear, and almost forty degrees. To have even a little break from the hellish winter we'd been having was a treat.

"Yeah, I like it," Bree said from the front seat. She navigated the on-ramp smoothly, and then we were on the highway, headed toward the nearby town of Greenport. Its downtown area had lots of cute shops and restaurants, and Bree had talked Robbie and me into an outing. After which I'd taken my nerve in both hands and called to invite Hunter to come, too. It wasn't exactly a date, but I was starting to feel more and more like we were a couple.

"Did you speak to the council about what we saw in the scrying stone?" I asked Hunter in a low voice.

He nodded. "I told Kennet Muir, my mentor. He promised the council would look into it. He warned me not to scry again, that it would only lead the dark wave to Mum and Dad. I know he's right, but . . ." He trailed off. I heard the impatience and frustration in his voice. I knew exactly how he felt. Even to know they were dead would in some ways be better than this constant state of limbo. I reached over and took his hand.

He turned to me, and we shared a look that seemed to melt my very soul. When had I ever felt so in tune with anyone?

"I know," he whispered, and I understood that he was saying he shared my feelings. My heart soared, and the bright day suddenly seemed almost too brilliant to bear.

Robbie turned around to look at me and Hunter. "Chip?" he offered, holding out the bag.

It was only ten-thirty in the morning, but I took a handful of barbecue-flavor potato chips and crunched them. With a particularly English look, Hunter declined. I hid a smile.

"Can I have a chip?" Bree asked.

Robbie fed one to her, watching her with an endearing combination of adoration and lust.

I ate another handful of chips and popped open a Diet Coke. Hunter gazed at me steadily, and I tried very hard not to think about making out with him on the floor of my room. "Nature's perfect beverage," I said, holding up the can. He grimaced and looked away.

"What an amazing day," Bree said, stretching in her seat.

"Thanks to me and my weather charm," I said lightly.

Robbie and Hunter both looked at me in alarm. "You didn't," said Robbie.

"You didn't," said Hunter.

I was enjoying this. "Maybe I did, maybe I didn't."

Hunter looked upset. "You can't be serious!"

Cahn't, I thought. Cahn too.

"Have you learned nothing these past weeks?" he asked. "Weather-working is not something to be taken lightly. You have no idea of the consequences this could have. How could you possibly have toyed with improper magick in this way?"

I met Bree's eyes in the rearview mirror. Instantly a smile broke across her face; she alone could tell I was teasing. It felt so wonderful to be driving somewhere again with her. The last three months had been desolate without her. We had a long way to go toward rebuilding our relationship, but we were making progress, and it felt great.

"You don't understand what the council—" Hunter went on, really getting wound up.

"Relax, Hunter," I said, taking pity on him. "I was just kidding. I don't even know how to work weather magick."

"Wha—what?" he sputtered.

"I don't even know how to work weather magick," I

repeated. "And I certainly have learned my lesson about the improper use of magick. Yes, sir. You won't catch me doing *that* again." I took a deep, satisfying swig of Diet Coke.

Hunter drummed his fingers on his door handle and looked out the window. After a moment a reluctant grin crept across his face, and I felt a burst of delight.

"By the way," he said a few minutes later, "I went into Selene's house and checked it out, looking for the source of that candle you saw. I didn't find any trace of anything, neither a person nor any magick."

"What candle at Cal's?" Robbie asked.

"I thought I saw someone holding a flickering candle in the window of Cal's old house," I explained.

Robbie looked startled and alarmed. "Yikes."

"So you didn't see footprints or anything?" I asked Hunter.

"No. It's already dusty inside, and the dust was undisturbed," Hunter said. "I wanted to have another go at getting into Selene's hidden library, but once again I couldn't find the door." He shook his head in frustration. "She has incredibly strong magick, I'll say that for her."

"Hmmm," I said, thinking. I had been in that library only once, by accident, when I had found Maeve's Book of Shadows. I wondered if I could get into it again. The International Council of Witches would surely want to see what, if anything, was left in that room. But I just couldn't face it. I never wanted to go in that house again. I wanted to help Hunter but just couldn't bring myself to offer to do this.

"Hey, Bree, you'll be getting off at the next exit," said Robbie, who was navigating.

"Okay," said Bree.

We didn't talk much about magick after that. I started thinking about the circle I'd had with Sky and Alyce yesterday. I knew I needed to learn more about my heritage, my birth parents, but I was at a loss as to where to begin. They'd died more than fifteen years before, and they'd known no one, had no close friends that I knew of, in America.

When I'd first found out that I was adopted, I'd read every newspaper article I'd found about the fire that killed my birth parents. I'd also found Maeve's Book of Shadows hidden in Selene's library (which probably should have tipped me off that Selene wasn't as open and giving as she seemed), and in the last few weeks I'd read it cover to cover. I'd even found secret passages detailing Maeve's passionate and tragic love affair with a man other than Angus, my birth father. I had Maeve's magickal tools, which she'd helped me to find through a vision.

But all that knowledge wasn't enough. It didn't fill in the gaping holes in my understanding of Maeve and Angus as *people*—and as Woodbane witches.

As I thought, the miles flew by, and then suddenly we were in Greenport, and Robbie was saying he was ready for lunch.

It was a happy, carefree day. We walked around, shopped, ate, laughed. I found a beautiful necklace of glass beads and twisted wire in a craft shop, and bought it to give Bree for Christmas, deciding on the spot to take the initiative. Someone had to be bold if we were going to put our friendship back together.

We all went home in the afternoon, and my aunt Eileen and her girlfriend Paula came over for dinner. Aunt Eileen, my mom's younger sister, is my favorite aunt, and I was glad to see them. I was even gladder to hear that they were settling into their new home. They'd recently moved to a house in the nearby town of Taunton, and at first they'd been harassed by a bunch of gay-bashing teenagers. Happily, those kids had been arrested, and the rest of the neighbors seemed to be going out of their way to make Aunt Eileen and Paula feel welcome.

At about eight-thirty I said my goodnights to everyone and headed out to my car. Our coven was having its weekly circle a day early this week, because a couple of people had holiday obligations with their families on Saturday night. The circle would be at Hunter and Sky's house.

The beautiful day had flowed into an equally beautiful winter evening. I felt I hadn't seen the stars for ages, and I relished looking at them through Das Boot's windshield.

"Morgan."

In one second my heart stopped cold. I slammed on the brakes, and my car swerved to the right. When I recovered, I wheeled around and scanned the backseat frantically, then looked at the seat next to me, which was of course empty. That voice. Quickly I reached over and pushed down all the door locks and peered out into the darkness.

It had been Cal, Cal's voice, calling me, as he had done many times before. A witch message. *Where was he?* He was searching for me. Was he nearby? My heart pounded, and adrenaline flooded my body so that my hands were shaky on the steering wheel. Cal! Oh Goddess. Where was he? What did he want?

My next thought was that I had to get to Hunter. Hunter would know what to do.

I sat for a moment, willing my body to stop trembling. Then I put my car back in gear and pulled out again onto the road. I cast my senses out as strongly as I could. I drove carefully, trying to interpret the feelings and impressions I got, but there was no Cal anywhere in them: no voice, no image, no heartbeat.

Cal. The instantaneous tug of my heart horrified and angered me. For one moment, when I'd heard his voice, my heart had leaped in eager anticipation. How stupid *are* you? I asked myself furiously. How big an idiot?

With my senses still at their most alert, I turned down Hunter's street and parked along his dark, weedy curb. Still no inkling of Cal's presence. But could I be sure my senses were correct? I cast a fearful look around me, then ducked through the opening in the hedge and headed up the narrow path to Hunter and Sky's ramshackle house.

A few feet from the front stairs the sound of voices and laughter from around back stopped me, and I picked my way impatiently through the dead grass and clumps of old snow, down the sloping lawn to their back porch. Hunter, I thought. I need you. I had made a mistake in not telling Hunter about the candle in Cal's house. This I knew I had to tell him right away.

"Yo! Morganita," Robbie called, and I looked up to see him hanging over the side of the deck. The house had been built into the side of a steep hill, so in front there were only four steps to the porch, but in back the porch was on the second story, supported by long wood pilings. Dropping off sharply behind the house, the hill turned into a steep, rocky ravine that was wild and beautiful during the day, dark and ominous at night.

"Hey," I called. "Where's Hunter?" I heard Bree's voice, and Jenna's laugh, and smelled the spicy, comforting scent of clove and cinnamon and apples.

"Right here," Hunter called.

I looked up at him, sending him a message. I need to talk to you. I'm scared.

Frowning, he started down to meet me. I hurried up the stairs, comforted by the reality of his presence. How far could someone send a witch message? I wondered. Was it possible Cal had called me from, say, France? I wanted to believe it was.

The porch staircase was long and rickety, with two turns before the top. Hunter was halfway down, and when I was almost to him, our glances met: we were both feeling the first prickle of alarm, our senses processing the unnatural feelings of shakiness and sway in the staircase. Then Hunter was reaching out his hand to me in slow motion, and I reached back even as I heard the first, thundering crack of wood splitting and felt the steps fall away beneath my feet, leaving me to drop endlessly into darkness, away from the light and my friends.

I was unconscious barely a moment: when I opened my eyes, wood fragments were still settling around me, and dust tickled my nose. I hurt all over.

"Morgan! Morgan! Hunter!" It was hard to tell who was calling, but I sensed Hunter near me, trying to struggle into a sitting position beneath one of the porch's support beams.

"Here!" Hunter called back, sounding shaken. "Morgan?"

"Here," I said weakly, feeling like my chest had been crushed, like I would never have enough breath in my lungs again. I tried to turn my head to look at the porch, but I must have rolled far down into the ravine, because I couldn't see the top.

"Hang on—I'll come get you," said Hunter, and I saw that he was about eight feet above me. Then Robbie, Matt, and Sky were leaning over the edge of the ravine with flashlights and a long rope. Holding the rope, Hunter edged his way toward me, and I grabbed his hand. Together we climbed up the rocky slope, and by the time I reached the top and sat down on the edge, I was trembling all over. I saw that the porch was still attached to the house, but the corner where the stairs had been sagged frighteningly, and the stairs themselves were in pieces. Our coven members stood on the lawn in a frightened group. It looked as if only Hunter and I had fallen when the stairs collapsed.

"Are you guys all right?" Bree asked. I saw fear and concern in her eyes.

I nodded. "Nothing feels broken. I must have landed on something soft," I said.

"That was me, I think. But I'm all right, more or less," Hunter added. He put a hand to his side and winced. "Just a few scrapes and bruises."

Sky put her arm around my waist and helped me around to the front of the house and inside.

"What happened?" Matt asked, following us. "Was the wood rotten?"

The coven members gathered around, going over what had just happened. As soon as they'd seen the stairs collapsing, they had crowded back through the kitchen door. I was so glad no one else had been hurt.

Sky left the kitchen, and Bree led me to a chair. "That was terrifying," she said. "Seeing you and Hunter go down." She shook her head.

"Here. I found some kava kava tea," said Jenna, pressing a warm mug into my hand.

I nodded and took it from her. "Thanks." I sipped the herb tea, hoping it would take effect soon. What a night it had been already, between hearing Cal's voice and then having this accident.

A few minutes later Sky came back in. "Hunter's looking at the porch," she reported. "Now let's get you cleaned up." She fetched a small basket of supplies from the bathroom and started washing my cuts and bruises. "Arnica," she said, holding out a small vial. "Good for trauma."

I was letting the pills dissolve under my tongue when Hunter limped in, his face grim. He had scrapes on his cheek, and his sweater was ripped and bloody on one side. For myself, I knew I'd have bruises on my back and legs, but that was pretty much it.

"The posts were sawed," Hunter announced, throwing down the coil of rope.

"What?" Robbie exclaimed. He, Bree, and Jenna were hovering by my chair. Matt, Raven, Sharon, and Ethan were standing at the back door, looking out at what was left of the porch. Thalia, Alisa, and Simon hadn't arrived yet.

I stared at Hunter in alarm, and Cal's voice echoed in my

head again. "Sawed with a saw, or spelled to break?" I asked.

"Looked like a saw," Hunter said as Jenna gave him a mug of the same tea I was drinking. "I didn't sense any magick. I'll have a closer look tomorrow, in the daylight."

He looked at me: we needed to talk. This was the second time we had almost been killed when we were together. It couldn't be coincidence.

"Maybe we should call the police," said Jenna.

Hunter shook his head. "They'd think we're subversive Wiccan weirdos who are being persecuted by the neighbors," he said dryly. "I'd rather not bring them into this."

"Okay, everybody, I'm going to lead the circle tonight," Sky announced, getting everyone's attention. "We'll start in a few minutes. Why don't the rest of you come to the circle room and start getting settled in while Morgan and Hunter finish their tea?"

They all trooped out. Robbie cast a worried glance over his shoulder at me as he left.

Alone, Hunter and I sat in silence for a moment.

"Neither of these accidents looked like magick," Hunter said at last. He breathed in the steam from his mug. "But as I said, I just can't think of any enemies I might have who aren't witches."

"What about someone who used to be a witch?" I asked, thinking of how David had been stripped of his magick. David was in Ireland, but Hunter must know other witches whose magick was bound.

"That's a thought," Hunter agreed, "although I pretty much know the location of the ones I've had to work against, and none of them are anywhere nearby." He put down his mug. "I'd better get cleaned up," he said, wincing as he stretched his arm. Automatically I followed him to the downstairs bathroom.

He snapped on the light. The room was small, unrenovated, with old-fashioned white tiles. It was scrupulously clean, and he started rummaging in the medicine cabinet. I perched on the edge of the tub. "I have something to tell you," I said.

He turned to look at me. "That sounds ominous." With careful movements he stripped off his dark, ripped sweater and the torn T-shirt underneath. Then he was wearing only his jeans, and I was trying not to stare at his naked, muscled chest. He was much fairer than Cal, his skin a smooth ivory color, and he had more chest hair than Cal. It was a golden brown and stretched from beneath his collarbone down in a V to where it disappeared into his pants, at eye level to where I was sitting. My mouth went dry, and I tried to focus on the large scrapes that sullenly oozed blood along his side.

When I dragged my eyes up to his face, he was looking at me with an almost glittering awareness. Wordlessly he handed me a wet washcloth, then held his arm away from his side.

Oh, I thought, standing up and starting to wash away the blood and dirt. My fingers tingled where they touched him. He turned for me, and I saw his back had been scraped as well, though not as badly. His skin was smooth, and he had pale freckles across both shoulders. I remembered that he was half Woodbane. He and Cal had the same father.

"Do you have a Woodbane athame?" I asked. "The birthmark?"

"I do, actually," he said. "Do you?"

"Yes." I dropped the washcloth in the sink and reached for the antibiotic ointment.

"I'll show you mine if you show me yours," he said with a wolfish smile.

Mine was under my left arm, on my side. Since I couldn't see his, I could only assume it was somewhere under his pants. My mind couldn't even begin to go there, so I said nothing.

"Don't you want to know where mine is?" he asked teasingly, and I could feel my blush starting at my neck and working its way upward. He leaned over me and brushed my hair over my shoulder, then traced my jawline with one finger. I remembered the way he felt, pressed against me, and most of my coherent thoughts fled.

"No," I said unconvincingly, lost in his eyes.

"I want to know where yours is," he breathed, his mouth close to mine.

The idea of his hands under my shirt, roaming over my skin, almost made my knees buckle. "Uh," I said, trying to talk myself out of whipping off my shirt right there. Focus. Come on, Morgan.

"Cal called me tonight," I blurted.

His hand fell away from my cheek. *"What?"* His voice reverberated loudly off the tiles.

"On my way over here. He sent me a witch message. I heard it in my head."

Hunter stared at me. "Why didn't you tell me right away?"

I just looked at him, and then he realized what had happened as soon as I got here.

"Right. I'm sorry. Well, what did he say? Could you tell where he was? Do you know where he is? Tell me everything." Moments before he had been playful and flirtatious; now he was intense, all business.

"There's nothing much to say," I explained. "I was driving here, and suddenly I heard Cal say, 'Morgan.' That's all. I was totally freaked and sent my senses out to find him but didn't feel him anywhere. I mean, I didn't feel a thing. And that was all he said."

"Do you know where he is?" Hunter demanded, holding my shoulders. "Tell me the truth."

"What do you mean? I *am* telling you the truth! I don't know where he is." I stared at him in bafflement. How could he think I might lie about something so important to both of us?

"Cal! That bastard," Hunter snapped, letting go of me. His hands clenched into fists, and the bathroom seemed too small to hold his rage. "Are you sure he didn't say anything else?"

"I'm positive. I already told you." I returned his glare. "Why are you treating me like a criminal? I didn't do anything wrong."

A muscle in his jaw flickered. But he didn't reply directly. Instead he shot questions at me like bullets. "Did you feel at all different? Is there a period of time you don't remember? Anything that feels confusing or odd?"

I realized what he was getting at. "Wouldn't I know if he'd put a spell on me?"

"No," Hunter said disdainfully. "He's a piss-poor witch, but he knows more than you do." He looked deeply into my eyes, as if he would see the spell reflected there. Then he turned away. I felt embarrassed and angry. Hunter was hurting my feelings, and I felt myself closing off to him. Especially when he wheeled back to me and added, "You're not holding anything back from me, are you? You're not feeling some idiotic urge to protect him because he's such a bloody stud and you still want him even after he tried to kill you?"

My mouth fell open, and my hand had shot up to slap him when it hit me: he was jealous. Jealous of my past with Cal. I stood there with my hand in the air as I tried to process this.

"Goddess, that bastard!" Hunter said. "If he's here, if I find him . . ."

Then what? I wondered. You'll kill him? I couldn't believe Hunter, cool, reserved Hunter had turned into this furious person I barely recognized in a matter of seconds. It frightened me.

"Hey, are you lot almost done in there?" Sky called from the other room.

"Yes," I called back, wanting to get away from Hunter. I wondered why on earth I had thought telling him would make me feel better or safer.

"This is one of the most useful rituals there is," said Sky almost half an hour later. I was finding that Sky's circle was different from any circle I'd attended: the fact was that whoever was leading a circle naturally imbued it with their aura, their power, and their whole persona. It was fascinating to see how different leaders cast different circles. So far I liked Sky's circle.

"I'd like to teach you how to deflect negative energy,"

said Sky. "This isn't something to use if you're under attack or in real trouble. It's more like something gentle and constant to surround yourself with in order to reduce negativity in your life and increase your positive energy."

I glanced at Hunter, thinking, He could use some positive energy right about now. His anger seemed less intense, but I could tell he was still brooding.

"It uses runes as its base," Sky explained. She took a small red velvet pouch from her belt and knelt. "Everyone sit down and come closer." Opening the pouch, she dumped its contents onto the wooden floor. Rune tiles spilled out, really pretty ones, made of different-colored stones. I had a rune set at home that I'd bought at Practical Magick, but mine was only fired clay. "There are so many different tools a witch can use. Incense, herbs, oils, runes or other symbols, crystals and gems, metals, candles." She grinned up at us as we crowded around her like kindergartners. "Witches are very practical. We use whatever we can find. Today we're using runes."

With deft fingers she organized the runes into three rows, each tile in line according to its place in the elder futhark, the traditional runic alphabet. We all knew the runes by heart at this point, and I could hear the coven members quietly identifying them.

"First we need eolh, for protection," said Sky, pulling it out of line. "What's another name for eolh?"

"Algiz," I said automatically.

"And wynn," she said, placing the wynn tile next to eolh. "For happiness and harmony. Another name for it?"

Simon said, "Wunjo."

"Uine," said Robbie, and Sky nodded. I liked how she was

involving everyone—she wasn't just lecturing, but including what little knowledge we had.

"Sigel, for sun, life, energy," said Sky, placing it by the other to form a triangle.

"Sowilo," said Thalia, looking pleased that she knew.

"Sugil," Bree added.

Sky grinned. "You guys are good. One more. Ur, for strength." She placed the tile for ur so that the four symbols together made a diamond shape.

"Uruz or uraz," said Raven, and her eyes met Sky's for a moment of private communion.

"Right. Now," Sky went on. "You can write these runes on a piece of paper, scratch them into an old slate or stone, carve them into a candle, or what have you. But use *these* four runes in *this* order. Put the written runes in your personal space, your bedroom, your car, even your school locker. When you see them, tap them with a finger and repeat, "Eolh, wynn, sigel, ur. Come to me from where you are. Guide the things I do or say, and let your wisdom come this way."

She sat back. "You can also circle your hand, palm down, three times deasil over the runes to help increase their power." She showed us. "That's all there is to it. It's not big magick or especially beautiful magick, but it's very useful magick."

"I think it's beautiful," said Alisa, looking young and sincere. "All magick is beautiful."

"No," I said, sounding more abrupt than I had meant to. "It isn't."

People looked at me, and I felt self-conscious. Hunter

and Sky nodded, and I knew they understood. We three had seen magick that was dark and ugly. It existed; it was all around us.

That night I found myself driving behind Bree on the way home from Hunter and Sky's. I felt shaken and upset, not to mentioned bruised and achy: hearing Cal's voice, the frightening fall I'd had, Hunter's awful reaction to hearing about Cal. Was Cal nearby? Just thinking about it terrified me. It was all too much. I just wanted to go home and get in bed and hold my kitten, Dagda.

Bree had taken the short route home, down Gallows Road. There were lots of twists and turns, but it took less time than going on main streets. Bree had always been the more daring driver of the two of us, and despite my trying to keep up, within minutes I lost sight of her in the darkness. Suddenly I was overwhelmed with the feeling of being completely alone on a dark road.

Without warning, my headlights flashed on something on the road ahead. I caught a blurry glimpse of something—a deer?—barely in time to slam on my brakes. As Das Boot screeched heavily to a halt, my eyes focused, and my mouth opened in a wordless, "Oh." My headlights shone on a figure who was walking toward my car, hands upraised.

Cal.

9.
Cal

Lammas, 1976

I'm fairly well settled into the house now that Clyda's gone. Her death three months ago was a surprise to everyone but me. She'd been sick, getting frailer and weaker. I think it was the dark wave in Madrid that really took it out of her. Really, she had no business traveling at her age. But it's difficult for some people to acknowledge their weaknesses.

I was in Ireland last week and met two interesting witches. One was a gorgeous boy, just old enough to shave, whose power is already frightening and strong and worth watching. I took Ciaran to bed for a night, and he was charmingly youthful, enthusiastic, and surprisingly skilled. I'm smiling even now, thinking about it.

But it's Daniel Niall who's haunting my thoughts,

and the irony of this can't escape me. Daniel is a Woodbane from England who came to one of Amyranth's gatherings in Shannon. I could see he was uncomfortable, had come out of curiosity and found us not to his liking. For some reason that made him even more attractive to me. He doesn't have Ciaran's harsh, raw beauty, but he is good-looking, with strong, masculine features, and when he looked into my eyes and smiled shyly, my heart missed a beat. Sweet Daniel. He's deeply good, honest, from one of those Woodbane covens that renounced evil ages ago. It's oddly endearing and also a challenge: how much more satisfying to seduce an angel than a villain?

—SB

At once I felt a wash of cold fear sweep over me from head to foot, and my hands clenched the steering wheel. Cal gestured with one hand, and Das Boot's engine died quietly and the headlights winked out. Automatically I began to use my magesight, the enhanced vision I'd been able to call on since shortly after I learned I was a blood witch.

Cal came closer, and I wrenched my door open and jumped out, determined to be standing during any meeting we had. When I saw his face, my breath left me, not in a whoosh but in a quiet trail, like a vine of smoke in the cold night air. Oh Goddess, had I forgotten his face? No—not when he haunted my dreams and my waking thoughts. But I had forgotten his impact on me, the sweet longing I felt when our eyes met, despite my fear.

Then of course came the remembered anger and a fierce rush of self-protective instinct.

"What are you doing here?" I demanded, trying to make my voice strong. But in the darkness I sounded harsh and afraid.

"Morgan," he said, and his voice crept along all my nerves, like honey. I had missed his voice. I hardened my heart and stared at him.

"Last time I saw you, you were trying to kill me," I said, striving for a flippancy I was too scared to pull off.

"I was trying to save you," he said earnestly, and came so close, I could see he wasn't an apparition, wasn't a ghost, but a real person in a real body that I had touched and kissed. "Believe me—if Selene had gotten her hands on you, death would have been far better. Morgan, I know now that I was wrong, but I was crazy with fear, and I did what I thought was best. Forgive me."

I couldn't speak. How did he do it? Even now, when I knew I should just jump in my car and drive away as fast as I could, my heart was whispering, Believe him.

"I love you more now than ever," Cal said. "I've come back to be with you. I told Selene I wouldn't help her anymore."

"You're telling me you've broken away from your mother?" I said. Emotion made my voice harsh, raw. "Give me one good reason I should believe you."

Wordlessly Cal opened his jacket. Underneath he wore a flannel shirt, and he unbuttoned the top three buttons and pulled it open so that I could see his chest. Instantly Hunter's naked chest flashed into my mind. Oh God, I thought with a tinge of hysteria.

Then I saw the blackened, burned-looking patch of skin directly over Cal's heart. I focused my magesight on it so that I could see clearly, despite the darkness. It was in the shape of a hand.

"Selene did that to me," Cal said, and remembered pain thrummed in his voice. "When I told her I chose you over her."

Goddess. I swallowed hard. And then, without allowing myself to think about what I was risking, I put out my hand and touched my fingers to his cheek. I had to know the truth.

His eyes flared open as he realized what I was doing, but he stood still. I pushed through the outer layers of his consciousness, feeling his resistance, feeling him will himself to accept my invasion. For the first time with Cal, I was controlling the joining of our minds. I would see what I wanted to see, not simply what he wanted to show me.

Then I was inside, and Cal was all around me. I saw my face, but the way he saw it, with a sort of glow around it that made me beautiful, unearthly. I was shaken to sense how much he wanted me.

I saw Hunter striding down the street in Red Kill, and felt an ugly burst of hatred and violence from Cal that rocked me.

I saw a steep hillside below me, dotted with small stucco houses with red roofs, that stretched down to a sparkling blue bay. I felt a breeze blowing against my cheeks. In the distance a red bridge stretched from one headland to another, and I realized I was seeing San Francisco, where I'd never been. It was beautiful, but it wasn't what I needed to see, so I kept searching.

Then I saw Selene.

She was looking directly at me, and I had to fight a strong impulse to hide my face, though I knew I was only seeing Cal's memory. She wasn't looking at me but at him. The expression in her eyes was cold fury.

"You can't go," she said. "I won't allow it."

"I am going," Cal said, and I felt his defiance, his fear, his resolve.

Selene's beautiful face twisted into a snarl of rage. "You idiot," she said. Then her hand was snaking toward him, so fast, it was just a blur, and I felt a searing pain as she touched Cal's flesh. Her hand felt deathly cold, as if it were made of liquid nitrogen, but then a wisp of smoke rose up in front of my eyes, and I smelled charred flesh. I cringed and gasped, twisting with Cal as he sought to escape the agony.

Then she took her hand away, and it was over, except for the memory of the pain.

"That was just the barest taste of what I can do," she said in a voice like iron. "I could have taken your heart as easily as plucking a cherry out of a bowl. I didn't because you are my son, and I know this foolishness will pass. But now you've experienced what I can do to those who cross me."

And she turned and strode away.

I let my hand drop, shaken, but Cal grabbed it. "Morgan, I need you. I need your love and your strength. Together we're strong enough to fight Selene, to win against her."

"No, we're not!" I cried. I snatched my hand away. "Are you insane? Selene could crush both of us and five other witches besides. I don't even know if she *can* be stopped."

"She can!" Cal said, coming closer still. He looked thinner than when I had seen him last, and his perpetual golden tan had faded slightly. I wondered if he had been eating, where he had been staying, and then told myself I didn't give a damn. "Selene can be stopped. The two of us, and your mother's coven tools, will be enough to stop her cold. I'm sure of it. Just tell me you'll work with me. Morgan, tell me you still love me." His voice dropped to a raspy whisper. "Tell me I haven't killed your love for me."

With a sense of shame I recognized that I cared for him, cared about him, that despite everything I didn't, couldn't hate him. But I couldn't say I still loved him, either, and there was no way I would agree to help him go up against Selene.

"There's no way we can be together now," I said, and the image of myself pressed against Hunter, kissing him fiercely, flashed into my mind.

"I know what I did to you was terrible," Cal said. "At first I was just trying to get next to your power. I admit that. But then I fell for you. Fell for your strength and beauty, your honesty and humility. Every time I saw you was a revelation, and now I can't live without you. I don't want to live without you. I want to be with you forever."

He looked so sincere, his face contorted with pain. I didn't know what to say: a thousand thoughts flew through my head like sparks flying upward from a fire. I recoiled from his presence even as part of me ached for his words to be true. I was scared of him and also afraid that what he was saying was real, that no one would ever love me so much again.

"All I ask is that you give me another chance," he pleaded in a tone that threatened to break my heart. "I was so horribly wrong—I thought I could have you and give

Selene what she wanted, too, but I couldn't. Please give me a chance to make it up to you, a chance to redeem myself. Morgan, please. I love you." He stepped closer still, and I could feel his breath, as cold as the night air, brushing against my cheek. "I don't want Selene to hurt you. Morgan, she wants to kill you. Now that she knows you'll never join her, she needs you dead so she can have your tools." He shook his head. "I can't let her do that."

"Where is she?" I asked shakily.

"I don't know," he said. "We were in San Francisco, but she's not there anymore. She's not far. I pick up on her sometimes. At least four members of her coven are with her. They're coming for you, Morgan. You have to let me protect you."

"Why should I trust you?" I demanded, trying to shut out the pain that seared my heart. "You tried to kill me once— why should I believe you won't just do it again?"

"Do you remember how good we were together?" Cal whispered, and I shivered. "Do you remember how we touched, how we kissed, how we joined our minds? It was so good, so right. You know it was real; you know I'm telling you the truth now. Please, Morgan . . ."

Part of me was no longer listening, my senses attuned to another vibration, another image. I looked down the road. "Hunter," I said before I thought.

Cal wheeled and looked down the road. I thought I could see the faintest stripe of light on the tree trunks. Headlights.

For an endless moment Cal and I looked at each other. He was just as breathtaking as he'd always been, with a new layer of vulnerability that he'd never had but that made him even more appealing. He was Cal, my first love, the one who'd opened new worlds to me.

"If you call me, I'll come," he said so softly, I could barely hear him.

"Wait!" I said. "Where are you staying? Where can I find you?"

He just smiled, and then he was running easily toward the woods that lined the road, and he faded between the trees like a wraith. I blinked, and he was completely gone, with no trace of ever having been there.

The headlights caught me in their glare, and I understood how a deer or rabbit could be pinned by them in terror. I stood by Das Boot, waiting for Hunter to stop.

"Morgan," he said, getting out of his car. Illogically, even after the scene in the bathroom, I felt almost like weeping with relief to see him. "Are you all right? Did something happen?"

My tongue pressed against my lips. Hunter was a Seeker. He had gone ballistic at the thought that Cal had even contacted me. If I told him I had just *seen* Cal, that Cal was nearby somewhere, Hunter wouldn't stop until he found Cal. And when he found him . . .

Hunter and Cal hated each other, had tried to kill each other. It was only luck that they *hadn't* killed each other. If Hunter found Cal now, one of them would die. That thought was completely unacceptable to me. I didn't know what to do about Cal, didn't know what to do about the knowledge that Selene was coming. All I knew was that I had to keep Hunter and Cal apart until I figured something out.

"I'm okay," I said, making my voice strong and sure. I chose my words carefully, knowing that he'd sense it if I lied outright. "I thought I almost hit a deer just now and stopped, but it's gone."

Hunter glanced at the woods, then he frowned slightly. "I sense something. . . ." he said, half to himself. He stood still for a moment, a listening expression on his face. Then he shook his head. "Whatever it was, it's gone now."

I kept my face blank.

He looked back at me. "I got an odd feeling about you," he said. "Like . . . panic."

I nodded, hoping he couldn't tell I was lying. "I thought I was going to crash. It's been kind of . . . an eventful day. I guess I freaked."

Hunter's frown cleared, and he looked contrite. "Are you sure you're okay?" he asked.

"Yeah." I started to get back in my car and prayed desperately that it would start, that Cal hadn't permanently disabled the engine. I couldn't believe I was lying so blithely to Hunter, Hunter who I had acknowledged was just about the only person I could trust. But I wasn't lying for me—I was trying to save Cal. And Hunter. I had to save them from each other.

Hunter leaned in the open doorway, bending to be at eye level with me. "Morgan—I'm sorry about the way I behaved earlier, in the bathroom. It's just—I'm upset about my father. I want to reach him and I can't. And I'm afraid for you. I feel that I need to protect you, and it kills me that I can't be with you all the time, making sure you're safe."

I nodded. "And that's why you want me to do the tàth meànma brach," I said.

"Yes." He paused. "Are you sore from the fall?"

"Yeah. I bet we'll both feel awful tomorrow. Especially you."

He laughed, and I turned my key. Das Boot's engine turned over at once.

"I'm going to get home now," I said unnecessarily. Quickly Hunter leaned in and kissed me, and then he stood back and shut my car door.

Had Cal seen that? I thought in panic. Oh Goddess, I hoped not. It would only infuriate him more. I drove off, looking back at Hunter in the mirror until I went around the next bend and I couldn't see him anymore. All I wanted to do was go home, curl up, and cry.

10.
Open

December 13, 1977

The mysteries of Amyranth can't hold a candle to the mysteries of love. What is it about Daniel Niall that makes me so crazy? Has he spelled me to love him? No— that's ludicrous. Noble, honest Daniel would never do such a thing. No, I love him for himself, and it's so out of character for me that I can't stop questioning it.

Why is he so compelling? How is he different from other men I've had? Like every other man, he's given in to me—no one has ever told me no, and Daniel is no exception. Yet I sense an inner wall that I can't breach. There's something within him that my love, my power, my beauty hasn't touched. What is it?

I know he loves me, and I know he wishes he didn't. I enjoy making him realize how much he wants me. I take *pleasure in watching him try to resist and being unable to. And then I make his compliance worth his while. But what is he holding back?*

At any rate, Daniel is here and there working on various studies—he's very academic; he wants to understand everything, know the history of everything. A real book witch. It takes him away from me often. Which is a good thing, because his presence severely curtails my Amyranth activities. I'm now doing more and more within the group and less with Turneval. The Unnamed Elders have begun teaching me the deeper magick of Amyranth, and it's more draining and exciting than anything I've imagined. I'm lost within it, drunk with it, immersed in it—and the only thing that pulls me out is the chance of spending time with Daniel. This makes me laugh.

—SB

That night I dreamed that Selene took on the form of a giant bird and snatched me off the school playing field, where, ludicrously, I was playing hockey with Hunter and Bree and Robbie. They stood on the grass, waving their hockey sticks helplessly, and I watched them get smaller and smaller as Selene bore me away. She took me to a giant nest perched on top of a mountain, and I looked down and saw Cal in the nest, and before my eyes he turned into a baby bird and gazed up at me with his sharp predator's beak gaping wide to engulf me. Then I woke up, drenched with sweat, and it was morning.

I spent the morning trying not to think about Cal. Three times I found myself picking up the phone to call Hunter, and three times I put the cordless handset back in its cradle. I felt too conflicted about what I would say.

"What's the matter, Morgan?" my mom asked as I prowled through the kitchen for the fourth time. "You seem so restless."

I forced myself to smile. "I don't know. Maybe I just need to go for a drive or something."

I grabbed my coat and car keys and headed out to Das Boot, not sure what my destination was. Then my senses tingled, and I knew Hunter was nearby. I felt a surge of elation and alarm as I saw him pull up in front of the house.

I walked over to his car, willing myself to seem calm, normal. He rolled down his window and peered out at me.

"We need to talk. Can I drive you somewhere?" he asked.

"Uh—I was just going for a drive," I mumbled. "I'm not really sure where."

"How about Red Kill?" he suggested. "I need to pick up some essential oils at Practical Magick. And you need to talk to Alyce."

So I climbed into his car and off we went.

"This morning Sky and I examined the porch supports more carefully," Hunter said as he drove. "They'd definitely been sawed, and we couldn't find any trace of magick."

"So what are you thinking?" I asked.

"I don't know," he said, tapping his fingers against the steering wheel.

I thought: had it been Cal? Had he been trying to kill

both me and Hunter at the same time? Had he cut Hunter's brake line as well? But why would he do it mechanically instead of with magick? Was I being a complete and total idiot by not telling Hunter that I'd seen Cal? I was so confused.

Alyce fed us lunch in her small apartment. I hadn't realized I was hungry until I smelled the beef stew that was filling the rooms with its rich scent. Hunter and I fell on it, and Alyce watched us, smiling. She sat at the table with us, not eating but sipping from a mug of tea.

"I've been considering your request for a tàth meànma brach," she said as I took a second slice of bread. "It's a serious thing, and I've given it a great deal of thought."

I nodded, my heart sinking at her tone. She was going to say no. I saw a glance pass between her and Hunter and felt my appetite fade away.

"You know, it can be very difficult," Alyce went on. "It would be very draining, both physically and emotionally, for both of us."

I nodded. I had asked too much.

"But I understand why you want to do this, why you asked me, and why Hunter also thinks it's a good idea," Alyce said. "And I've come to agree. I think that you're a target of Selene's group, and I think you need more protection than others can provide for you. The best kind of protection comes from within, and by joining with me and learning what I know, you will be much stronger, much more capable of defending yourself."

I looked at her with hope. "Does that mean—"

"You'll need to free yourself of as many mental distractions as you can," Alyce said gently. "And there are some ritual preparations you'll need to make. Hunter and Sky can help you with them. Let's do it soon—the sooner the better. Tomorrow evening."

Back in Hunter's car, on our way to my house, I could hardly sit still. The idea of being able to absorb all of Alyce's considerable learning, all in one day, was exhilarating and nerve-racking.

"Thank you for speaking to Alyce for me," I said. "Encouraging her to do the tàth meànma brach."

"It was her decision." He sounded remote, and I felt a surge of frustration about our relationship. It struck me for the first time that Hunter and I were similar, and that was why we clashed so much. With Cal it had been clear, easy—he had been the pursuer and I the pursued, and that had worked well with my shyness and insecurity. But both Hunter and I would be more comfortable if the other person were taking charge. At this point I had to assume there was some reason why we had kissed each other, and not just once or twice. Hunter wasn't the kind of person who would do that lightly, and neither was I. So what were we doing? Were we falling in love?

I have to lay myself on the line, I realized with a flash of perfect clarity. If I want to go deeper with him, I have to open myself to him and trust that he doesn't want to hurt me. And I do want to go deeper with him.

But first . . . but first I had to tell him about Cal. It was too huge a secret between us. Nor was it my secret to keep.

Hunter was in danger from Cal as much, maybe even more than I was. I would have to tell him and hope that he wouldn't let his emotions overtake his good sense.

I swallowed hard. Do it, I told myself. Do it!

"I saw Cal last night," I said quietly.

Next to me Hunter went rigid, his hands clenching the steering wheel. He glanced quickly right and left, then swung the car onto a dirt road that I hadn't even seen. We bumped over rocks and frozen mud before coming to a halt about twenty feet off the main road.

"When?" Hunter demanded, turning off the engine and facing me. He unclipped his seat belt and leaned toward me. "When?" he repeated. "Was it when I saw you on the road?"

"Yes," I admitted. "It wasn't a deer I saw. It was Cal. He was standing in the road, and he held up his hand and my car went dead."

"What happened? What did he do to you?"

"Nothing. We just talked," I said. "He said he came back to Widow's Vale to be with me. He told me he's broken away from Selene."

"And you believed that load of crap?" Hunter exclaimed. His eyes blazed.

My chin came up. "Yes." His contemptuous tone made me feel small, hurt. "I did tàth meànma with him. He's telling the truth."

"Goddess." Hunter spat out the word. "How could you be so bloody stupid? You've done tàth meànma with him before, and he still managed to fool you."

"But I controlled it this time!" I cried.

"You *think* you did. Why did you lie to me?" His eyes narrowed. "He *has* put a spell on you!"

Remembering how it had felt when Cal had put a spell on me made me shiver. "No. I just—I had just told you about his witch message, and you freaked out, and I thought if I told you he was right there, you guys would—would fight, and it made me sick to think about."

"You're damn right I freaked out!" Hunter said, raising his voice. "Good God, Morgan, we've been looking for Cal and Selene for three weeks now! And all of a sudden you say, guess what? I know where he is! I mean, what the hell kind of game are you playing?"

I hated the way he was looking at me, as if he were questioning his trust of me—if he had ever trusted me at all, and to my horror, I started crying. I don't cry easily in front of people, and I would have given up a lot to have not cried then, but everything crashed down on me all at once, and I crumbled.

"I'm not playing games!" I said, dashing my tears away. "I'm just confused, just human! I loved Cal, and I don't want you two to kill each other!"

"You're not *just* human, Morgan," Hunter said. "You're a witch. You have to start living up to that fact. What do you mean, you loved Cal? What has that got to do with anything? He tried to kill you! Are you stupid? Are you blind?"

"It wasn't all his fault!" I yelled, seeing the blazing fury in Hunter's eyes. "You know that, Hunter. He grew up with Selene for eighteen years. What would you have been like in that situation?" I took a couple of quick, hard breaths, trying to get hold of myself. "I'm not blind. Maybe

I am stupid. Mostly I'm just confused and scared and tempted."

He narrowed his eyes, seizing on my words like a snake does a rat. "Tempted? Tempted by what? The dark side? Or by Cal? Is that it? Are you saying you still love him?"

"No! Yes! Stop twisting my words! All I'm saying is that I loved him, and I thought he loved me, and I haven't forgotten that!" I shouted. "He introduced me to magick. He made me feel beautiful!" I abruptly shut up, breathing hard.

Heavy silence filled the car. I sensed Hunter striving to rein in his anger. What am I doing? I thought miserably.

Then his face softened. I felt his hand at my neck, brushing my hair back, stroking my skin. My breath caught in my throat, and I turned to him.

"I'm sorry," I whispered. My skin felt like it was on fire where his fingers passed over it.

"What do you want? I know you were happy with Cal, and I want you to be happy with me. But I'm not Cal, and I never will be," he said, his face close to mine. His voice was soft. "If you want me, then tell me. I need you to tell me."

My eyes widened. Cal had always been almost forceful, the one who decided, cajoled, seduced. Why was Hunter asking me to make myself vulnerable?

As if reading my thoughts, he said, "Morgan, I can tell you and show you what I want. But if *you* don't know what you want, I don't want to go there. *You* need to know what you want, and you need to be able to tell me and show me." His eyes were wide, vulnerable, his lips were warm and close to mine.

Oh my God, I thought.

"It's not enough for you to let me want you," he went on. "I need you to actually want me back and to be able to show me that. I need to be wanted, too. Do you see what I mean?"

I nodded slowly, processing a hundred thoughts.

"Can you give me that?"

My eyes felt huge as I wondered if I could—if I was brave enough. I didn't speak.

"Right, then." He pulled back, my body saying, no, no, and then he started the car, carefully backed up, and we went back to Widow's Vale. In front of my house he stopped and turned to look at me again.

"I have to look for Cal," he said. "You know that, don't you?"

I nodded reluctantly. "Don't hurt him," I said in a near whisper.

"I can't promise that," he told me. "But I'll try. Will you think about what I said?"

I nodded again.

Hunter took my chin in his hand and kissed me hard and fast on the mouth, not once but again and again, hungrily, and I made a little sound and opened my mouth to him. Finally he pulled back, breathing hard, and we looked at each other. He put the car into gear again. I climbed out in a daze and headed up my front walk.

11.
The Graveyard

Beltane, 1979

I've been married for less than twenty-four hours, and already my new husband is threatening to leave me—he thinks the ceremony was all my doing, it wasn't what he expected, I didn't respect his wishes, etc. He'll be all right. He needs to calm down, to relax, to get over his fears. Then we can talk, and he'll see that everything is all right, everything is fine, and we were meant to be together.

Why did I marry Daniel Niall? Because I couldn't help myself. Because I wanted him too much to let him go. Because I needed to be the one he wanted, the one he would live with and come home to. My mother would have approved of this match. Anyone who actually knows me thinks I'm crazy. At any rate, Daniel and I were married last night, and for me it was beautiful, powerful, primal.

When we stood, sky clad, under the ripe, full moon, with Turneval chanting around us, the heady scent of herbs burning, the warmth of the bonfire toasting our skin—I felt like the Goddess herself, full of life, fertile. For me it was so natural that we embrace, open our mouths and kiss, that I press myself against him. And how could he not respond? We were naked, I was seducing him, it was a full moon. Of course he responded. But he found his physical response (so public, so witnessed) to be unbearable. For Daniel it was humiliation, abasement.

How will I reconcile these two areas of my life? How can I keep my work with Amyranth a secret? How can I protect Daniel from Amyranth?

I'll have to solve the problems as they come.

—SB

On Sunday, I once again skipped church and tried to ignore my mother's disapproving looks. She and my dad tried to talk me into meeting them for lunch at the Widow's Vale Diner afterward, but I was fasting to purify my body for my upcoming tàth meànma brach with Alyce, so I declined. Instead, I stayed in my room, meditating. Alyce had recommended that I spend at least three hours meditating on the day of the ritual to cleanse my spirit and my psyche of negative patterns and clutter, for lack of a better word.

By eleven o'clock, I was starving. My stomach cried out for Diet Coke and a Pop-Tart, but I resisted, feeling virtuous.

At noon I'd just pulled out my altar when Hunter called.

He told me in a neutral way that he'd gone to Cal and Selene's old house and one or two other places to see if he could find Cal, but he'd had no luck. "I know he's been there—I can feel traces of him," Hunter said. "But everywhere I go, he's moved on, and I can't tell where he's gone. I didn't think he was skilled enough to hide his trail from me once I'd picked up a trace of him, but he seems to be."

I decided it was time to change the subject. "I can't believe the tàth meànma brach is tonight," I said. "I'm kind of nervous. Should I be?"

"Yes," Hunter said. "But come over to my house at three, and we'll help you get ready. You've got to drink the tea, then take the ritual bath so that you'll be fully cleansed. And you'll need to wear a green linen robe—Sky's got one. Tell your mum and dad you're having dinner with us and you won't be home until fairly late."

"Okay," I said, feeling scared and uncertain.

His voice softened. "You'll be all right, Morgan," he said. "You're strong. Stronger than you know."

After we said goodbye and hung up, I went back to my room. I opened a spell book that Alyce had loaned me and began to read through the purification spell she'd marked, but my stomach kept distracting me. All of a sudden, when I was trying so hard not to think about food, I had a realization: my brain was still incredibly cluttered with Cal. I thought about him, wondered about him, dreamed about him.

Then I realized I had to talk to him, find out once and for all where we stood. I had to put all my feelings toward him to rest or I would never be able to move forward, and I couldn't take part in the tàth meànma brach. I had to get closure somehow, put an end to all my confusion about him.

I knew I was doing something that could be dangerous. But I also knew I had to do it. Before I could change my mind, I drove over to the old Methodist cemetery, the place where my former coven, Cirrus, had celebrated Samhain. The place where Cal had kissed me for the first time.

It was another clear, cold day, sunny with a wintry brightness and almost no wind. Sitting on the old tombstone we had once used as our altar, I felt almost shaky with nervousness and adrenaline and lack of food. Would Cal come? Would he try to hurt me again? There was no way to know except by calling him. Closing my eyes, trying to ignore the rumbling of my stomach, I sent a witch message to him. *Cal. Come to me, Cal.* Then I sat back and waited.

Before, when I had called Cal, he had usually come within minutes. This time the wait seemed endless. My butt had turned numb on the cold stone before he appeared, gliding silently between the overgrown juniper trees. My eyes registered his appearance, and I was glad it was broad daylight and that I wasn't alone on a dark road.

"Morgan." His voice was soft as a breeze, and I felt it rather than heard it. He walked toward me with no sound, as if the dried leaves underfoot were silenced. I was drawn to his beautiful face, which was both guarded and hopeful.

"Thanks for coming," I said, and I suddenly knew without a doubt that he'd been waiting, scanning the area, making sure I was alone. The last time we were in this place, he had overpowered me and kidnapped me in my car. This time, despite some lingering fear, I felt stronger, more prepared. This time, too, I was ready to call Hunter at a moment's notice.

"I was so glad to hear from you," he said, coming to stand in front of me. He reached out and put his hands on my knees, and I drew back from the familiarity. "There's so much I need to talk to you about. So much I need to tell you, to share with you. But I didn't know how much much Giomanach had influenced you." He spat Hunter's coven name, and I frowned.

"Cal, I need to know," I said, getting to the point. "Have you really broken away from Selene? Do you really want to stop her?"

He again put his hands on my knees. They felt warm through my jeans, against my cold flesh. "Yes," he said, leaning close. "I'm finished with Selene. She's my mother, and I always had a son's loyalty to her. That's not hard to believe, is it? But now I see that what she does is wrong, that it's wrong for her to call on the dark side. I don't want any part of it. I choose you, Morgan. I love you."

I pushed his hands off my knees. His brow darkened.

"I remember when you didn't push me away," he said. "I remember when you couldn't get enough of me."

"Cal," I began, and then my anger pushed ahead of my compassion. "That was before you tried to kill me," I said, my voice strong.

"I was trying to save you!" he insisted.

"You were trying to control me!" I countered. "You put binding spells on me! If you had been honest about what Selene wanted, I could have made my own decision about what to do and how to protect myself. But you didn't give me that chance. You wanted all the power; you wanted to decide what was best." As soon as I said that, I realized it was true, and I realized that I had never absolutely trusted Cal, never.

"Morgan," he began, sounding infuriatingly reasonable, "you had just discovered Wicca. Of course I was trying to guide you, to teach you. It's one of the responsibilities of being an initiated witch. I know so much more than you— you saw what happened with Robbie's spell. You were a danger to yourself and others."

My mouth opened in fury, and he went on, "Which doesn't mean I don't love you more than you can imagine. I do, Morgan, I do. I love you so much. You complete me. You're my mùirn beatha dàn, my soul's other half. We're supposed to be together. We're supposed to make magick together. Our powers could be more awesome than anything anyone's ever seen. But we have to do it together."

I swallowed. This was so hard. Why did it still hurt so much, after all Cal had done to me? "No, Cal. We're not going to be together. We're not mùirn beatha dàns."

"That's what you think now," he said. "But you're wrong."

I looked deeply into his golden eyes and saw a spark of what looked like madness. Goddess! My blood turned to ice, and I felt incredibly stupid, meeting him here alone.

"Morgan, I love you," Cal said cajolingly. He stepped closer to me, his eyes hooded in the look that had never before failed to make me melt inside. "Please be mine."

My breath became more shallow as I wondered how to extricate myself from this. This Cal wasn't the Cal I had known. Had that person ever existed? I couldn't tell. All I knew was that now, here, I had to get away from him. He frightened me. He *repulsed* me.

Just like that, like extinguishing a candle with my fingertips, my leftover love for him died. I felt it in my heart, as if a dark shard of glass had been pulled out, leaving a bleeding wound. My throat closed and I wanted to cry, to mourn for the death of the naive Morgan who had once been so incredibly happy with this falsehood.

"No, Cal," I said. "I can't."

His face darkened, and he looked at me. "Morgan, you're not thinking clearly," he said, a tone of warning in his voice. "This is me. I love you. We're lovers."

"We were *never* lovers," I said. "And I don't love you."

"Morgan, listen to me," Cal said.

"You're too late, Sgàth," said Hunter's voice, cold and hard, and Cal and I both jumped. How had he come up without our feeling it?

"There's nothing for you to hunt here, Giomanach," Cal spat. "No lives for you to destroy, no magick you can strip away."

I felt a wave of power welling up from Cal, and I scrambled off the tombstone. I had once been caught between Cal and Hunter during a battle. I didn't want to go through it again.

"Hunter, why are you here?" I asked.

"I felt something dark here. I came to investigate," he said tightly, not taking his eyes off Cal. "It's my job. It was you who cut the brakes in my car, wasn't it, Sgàth? You who sawed through the stair supports."

"That's right." Cal grinned at Hunter, a feral baring of teeth. "Don't you wonder what else is waiting for you?"

"Why didn't you use magick?" Hunter pressed. "Is it because without Selene, you have nothing of your own? No power? No will?"

Cal's eyes narrowed, and his hands clenched. "I didn't use magick because I didn't want to waste it on you. I am much stronger than you will ever be."

"Only when you're with Morgan," Hunter said coldly. "Not on your own. You're nothing on your own. Morgan knows that. That's why she's here."

I started to say it was *not,* but Cal turned on me. "You! You lured me here, to turn me in to him."

"I wanted to talk to you!" I cried. "I had no idea Hunter would be here."

Hunter turned his implacable gaze on me. "How could you go behind my back after all we've talked about?" he asked in a cold, measured voice. "How could you still love *him?*" He flung out his hand at Cal.

"I don't love him!" I screamed, and in the same instant Cal threw up his hands and began to chant a spell. The language he used was unfamiliar, ugly, full of guttural sounds.

Hunter let out a low growl. I sucked in my breath as I saw that his athame was in his hand, the single sapphire in its hilt flashing as it caught the late winter sun. Stepping back, I saw how he and Cal were facing each other, saw the violence ready to erupt. Damn them! I couldn't go through this again, not Cal and Hunter trying to kill each other, myself frozen, an athame leaving my hand and sailing through the intense cold. . . .

No. That was another time, another place. Another Morgan. I felt power rise inside me like a storm. I had to put an end to this. I had to.

"Clathna berrin, ne ith rah." The ancient Celtic words poured from my lips, and I spat them into the daylight. Hunter and Cal both spun to look at me, their eyes wide. "Clathna ter, ne fearth ullna stàth," I said, my voice growing stronger.

"Morach bis, mea cern, cern mea." I knew exactly what I was doing but couldn't tell where it was coming from or how I knew it. I snapped my arms open wide, to encompass both of them, and watched with a strange, fierce joy as their knees buckled and they sank, one at a time, to the ground. "Clathna berrin, ne ith rah!" I shouted, and then they were on their hands and knees, helpless against the force of my will.

Goddess, I thought. I felt like I was outside myself, watching this strange, frightening being who controlled the gravity of a world with her fingertips. My right hand outstretched to keep Cal in place, I slowly moved toward Hunter.

He didn't speak, but when I saw the blazing fury in his eyes, I knew I couldn't release him yet. I pointed at him. "Stand up," I commanded. When I raised my hand, he was able to stand, like a puppet. "Get in my car."

Stumbling like an automaton, Hunter headed for Das Boot. I walked backward, following him, keeping Cal under my power. Hunter climbed clumsily into the passenger seat, and I fished out my keys with my left hand. Then I drew some sigils in the sky, sigils I didn't remember learning, that would keep Cal in place until we were well away.

Then I leaped into the driver's seat, jammed the keys into the ignition, stomped on the gas, and got the hell out of there.

I released Hunter after I had parked in front of his house and felt the sudden tightening of his muscles as he took control of them again.

I was afraid to look at him, scared even to think about what I'd done. It was as if I'd been taken over by my power, as if the magick had controlled me instead of the other way around. Or was I just trying to make excuses for having done something unforgivable?

I felt the burning fury of Hunter's gaze on me. He slammed the car door and walked unsteadily up to his house. I felt weak and headachy from lack of food and too much magick, but I knew I needed to talk to Hunter. I got out of Das Boot and followed him into the house.

Inside, Sky looked up as I came in, and seeing my troubled expression, she pointed wordlessly up the stairs. I'd been upstairs once before but hadn't really taken in any details. Now I looked into one room: it was Sky's, or at least I hoped it was since there was a black bra draped across the bed. I walked past a small bathroom with black-and-white tile flooring and then came to the only other room and knew it must be Hunter's bedroom. The door was ajar, and I pushed it open without knocking: daring Morgan.

He lay across his bed, staring at the ceiling, still wearing his leather jacket and his boots.

"Get out," he said without looking at me.

I didn't know what to say. There was nothing I could say right now. Instead I dropped my coat onto the floor and walked to the bed, which was just a full-size mattress and box spring stacked on the floor, neatly made up with a threadbare down comforter.

Hunter tensed and looked at me in disbelief as I lowered myself next to him. I thought he was going to push me right off the bed onto the floor, but he didn't move, and hesitantly I edged closer to him till I was lying by his side. I put my head on his shoulder and curled myself up next to him, with my arm draped over his chest and my leg across his. His body was rigid. I closed my eyes and tried to sink into him. "I'm so sorry," I murmured, praying that he would let me stay long enough to really apologize. "I'm so sorry. I didn't know what else to do. I didn't know what was going to happen. I just couldn't bear to see you hurt each other—or worse. I'm sorry."

It was a long time before he relaxed at all and longer still before his hand came up to stroke my hair and hold me close to him. It was starting to get dark outside, it was late, and I hadn't yet drunk the special herb tea I was supposed to drink before my tàth meànma brach. But I lay there with Hunter slowly stroking my hair, feeling like I had found a special sort of refuge, a safe haven completely different from what I had experienced with Cal. I didn't know if Hunter would ever be able to forgive me; I had never been able to truly forgive Cal for doing the same thing to me. But I hoped that somehow Hunter was a bigger person than I was, a better person, and would find a way not to hold this against me forever.

It was then I realized how incredibly important his opinion of me was, how much his feelings mattered to me, how desperately I wanted him to care for me, admire me, the way I cared for and admired him.

Finally I took a deep breath and said, "I love you. I want you. This is right."

And Hunter said, "Yes," and he kissed me, and it was as if a universe unfolded within me. I felt infinite, timeless, and when I opened my eyes and looked at Hunter, he was outlined in a blaze of golden light, as if he were the sun itself.

Magick.

12.
The Brach

February 27, 1980

Daniel is in England again. He's been gone two weeks, and I'm not sure when he'll be back. He always comes back, though. The temptation is strong to cast a summoning spell on him, pulling him to me sooner, but I have resisted, and there's a satisfaction in knowing that he always comes back because he can't help himself and not because I forced him to.

Is this marriage? This isn't my parents' marriage, quiet and sedate and tandem. When Daniel and I are together, we are shouting, arguing, fighting, and despising each other, and then we are grappling, falling to the bed, making love with intense passion that has as much to do with hate as it does with love. And then in the aftermath I see his beauty once again, not just his physical beauty, but *his inner sweetness, the goodness inside him. I love and appreciate that, even as it clashes so harshly with what is inside me.*

We have moments of calm and gentleness, during which we're holding hands and kissing sweetly. Then Amyranth raises its head or his studies call him away, and we are again two angry cats tied in a burlap bag and thrown into a river: desperate, clawing, fighting, trying only to survive no matter the cost. And he goes away and I immerse myself in Amyranth, and I know I could never give it up. Then I miss Daniel and he comes back, and the cycle starts again.

Is this marriage? It is my marriage.

—SB

I'm not sure how long I lay with Hunter. Eventually his even breathing told me he was asleep. I didn't think he had forgiven me just because I had told him I loved him and he had kissed me. Was I fickle, to love someone else so soon after Cal? Was I setting myself up for another heartbreak? Did Hunter love me? I felt he did. But I had no idea whether we had a future, where our relationship would lead us, how long it would last. These questions would have to wait: now it was time, past time, for me to prepare for the tàth meànma brach.

Moving quietly, I uncoiled myself and left the room. Holding my shoes in one hand, I went downstairs. Sky was in the kitchen, reading the newspaper and drinking something hot and steaming in a mug. She looked at me expectantly.

"I'll explain it all later," I told her, feeling very tired.

"It's late," she said after a moment. "Almost five o'clock. I'll fix you your special tea." She made me a huge pot of it, and I started drinking it obediently. It tasted like licorice and wood and chamomile and things I couldn't identify.

"What does this tea do?" I asked, finishing the mug.

"Well . . . ," said Sky.

I found out before she finished speaking. The secret of the herbal tea was that it was a system cleanser and basically finished off the effects of the fasting and the water drinking. I doubled over as I felt my stomach cramp. Sky, trying not to smirk, pointed to the downstairs bathroom.

In between bouts of, ahem, gut emptying, I meditated and talked to Sky. I told her what had happened with Cal, and she listened with surprising compassion. I wondered—hoped—that my binding spell had worn off and he wasn't still stuck in the cemetery in the cold. It must have. Where was he now? How angry was he? Had he felt my love for him die, the way I had?

Sky asked at some point, "How are you feeling?"

"Empty," I said bleakly, and she laughed.

"You'll be glad of it later," she said. "Trust me. I've seen people do a brach without cleaning out their systems and fasting, and they truly regretted it."

I sniffed the air. "What's that?"

"Lasagna," Sky admitted. "It's almost seven."

"Oh, Jesus," I moaned, feeling hollow and starving and exhausted.

"Here," Sky said briskly, holding out a bundle of pale

green linen. "This is for you. I've drawn you a bath upstairs and put in some purifying herbs and oils and things. Have a good soak in the tub, and you'll feel better. Afterward put this on, with nothing underneath. Also, no knickers, no jewelry, no nail polish, nothing in your hair. All right?"

I nodded and headed up the stairs. Hunter was in the upstairs bathroom, putting out a rough, unbleached towel. I had showered here once before, but now it felt bizarrely intimate, taking a bath in his house—especially so soon after we had been kissing on his bed. I felt myself blush, and he gave me an unreadable look and left the room, closing the door behind him.

The bathroom looked lovely, very romantic, with all the lights off and candles burning everywhere. Steam rose from the water in the claw-foot tub, and there were violet petals floating on it, and rosemary, and eucalyptus. I shimmied out of my clothes and sank blissfully into the hot water. I don't know how long I lay there, my eyes closed, inhaling the fragrant steam and feeling the tension draining away. There was a fine grit of salt lining the bottom of the tub, and I rubbed it into my skin, knowing it would help purify me and dispel negative energy.

I felt Sky coming closer, and then she tapped on the door and said, "Ten minutes. Alyce will be here soon."

Quickly I grabbed the homemade soap and a washcloth and scrubbed myself all over. Then I shampooed my hair. I ran fresh water and rinsed myself off well, then rubbed hard with the rough towel until I was dry. I felt like a goddess; clean, light, pure, almost ethereal. The horrible events of the day receded, and I felt ready for anything, as if I could wave my hand and rearrange the stars in the sky.

I untangled my long, damp hair with a wooden comb I found, then put on the green robe. At last I floated downstairs barefoot to find Alyce, Sky, and Hunter waiting for me in the circle room. I paused uncertainly in the doorway, and the first thought I had was, Hunter knows I'm naked under this. But nothing in his face betrayed that knowledge, and then Alyce was walking toward me, her hands outstretched, and we hugged. She was wearing a lavender robe very similar to mine, and her hair was down for once, silver and flowing halfway down her back. She looked serene, and I was so grateful to her for doing this.

Sky and Hunter both came forward and hugged each of us, and I was acutely aware of how his lean body felt against mine. I noticed that he had already started drawing circles of power on the floor. There were three: a white one of chalk, then one made of salt, and then an inner one of a golden powder that smelled spicy, like saffron. Thirteen white pillar candles ringed the outer circle, and Alyce and I walked through the circle openings. We sat cross-legged on the floor, facing each other, smiling into each other's eyes as Hunter closed the circles and chanted spells of protection.

"Morgan of Kithic and Alyce of Starlocket, do you agree to enter knowingly and willingly into a tàth meànma brach here tonight?" asked Sky formally.

"Yes," I said, and nervousness bubbled up inside me. Was I really ready? Could I accept Alyce's knowledge? Or would I end up going blind, like that witch Hunter had told me about?

"Yes," Alyce said.

"Then let's begin," said Hunter. He and Sky drew back

from the circles and sat leaning against cushions by a far wall. I got the impression they were like spotters who would jump in and help us if anything weird happened.

Alyce reached out with her hands and put them on my shoulders, and I did the same to her. We leaned our heads over until our foreheads touched lightly, our eyes still open. Her shoulders felt warm and smooth and round under my hands; I wondered if I felt bony, raw, under hers.

Then, to my amazement, she started chanting my own personal power spell, the one that had come to me weeks ago.

> "An di allaigh an di aigh
> An di allaigh an di ne ullah
> An di ullah be nith rah
> Cair di na ulla nith rah
> Cair feal ti theo nith rah
> An di allaigh an di aigh."

My voice joined hers, and we sang it together, the ancient rhythm flowing through our blood like a heartbeat. My heart lifted as we sang, and I saw joy on Alyce's face, making her beautiful, her violet-blue eyes full of wisdom and comfort. We sang, two women, joined by power, by Wicca, by joy, by trust. And slowly, gently, I became aware that the barriers between our minds were dissolving.

The next thing I was aware of was that my eyes were closed—or if they weren't closed, I was no longer seeing things around me, was no longer conscious of where I was. For a moment I wondered with panic if I were blind, but then I lost myself in wonder. Alyce and I were floating, joined, in a sort of nether space where we could simultane-ously see everything and nothing. In my mind Alyce held out her hands and smiled at me, saying, "Come."

My muscles tensed as I seemed to be drawn toward an electrified wormhole, and Alyce said, "Relax, let it come," and I tried to release every bit of resistance I had. And then . . . and then I was inside Alyce's mind: I was Alyce, and she was me, and we were joined. I took in a sharp breath as waves and waves of knowledge swept toward me, cresting and peaking and lapping against my brain.

"Let it come," Alyce murmured, and again I realized I had tensed up and again I tried to release the tension and the fear and open myself to receive whatever she gave. Reams of sigils and characters and signs and spells crashed into me, chants and ancient alphabets and books of learning. Plants and crystals and stones and metals and their properties. I heard a high-pitched whimpering sound and wondered if it was me. I knew I was in pain: I felt like I wore a helmet of metal spikes that were slowly driving into my skull. But stronger than the pain was my joy at the beauty around me.

Oh, oh, I thought, unable to form words. Flowers spun toward me through the darkness, flowers and spiked woody branches and the scents of bitter smoke, and suddenly it was all too intense, and bile rose in my throat, and I was glad I had nothing in me to throw up.

I saw a younger, brown-haired Alyce wearing a crown of laurel leaves as she danced around a maypole as a teenager. I saw the shame of failed spells, charms gone wrong, a pan-icked mind blanking before a teacher's stern rebuke. I felt flames of desire licking at her skin, but the man she desired faded away before I saw who he had been, and something in me knew he had died, and that Alyce had been with him when he had.

A cat passed me, a tortoiseshell cat she had loved profoundly, a cat who had comforted her in grief and calmed her in fear. Her deep affection for David Redstone, her anguish and disbelief at his betrayal swirled through me like a hurricane, leaving me gasping. Then more spells and more knowledge and more pages and pages of book learning: spells of protection, of ward evil, of illusion, of strength. Spells to stay awake, to heal, to help in learning, to help in childbirth, to comfort the ailing, the grieving, the ones left behind when someone dies.

And scents: throughout it all the scents roiled through me, making me gag and then inhale deeply, following a tantalizing scent of flowers and incense. There was smoke and burned flesh and oils gone bad; there was food offered to the Goddess, food shared with friends, food used in rituals. There was the metallic tang of blood, coppery and sharp, that made my stomach burn, and wretched odors of sickness, of unhealed flesh, of rot, and I was panting, wanting to run away.

"Let it come," Alyce whispered, and her voice cracked.

I wanted to say something, say it was too much, to slow it down, to give me time, that I was drowning, but no words came out that I could hear, and then more of Alyce's knowing came at me, swept toward me. Her deep, personal self-knowledge flowed over me like a warm river, and I let myself go into it, into the power that is itself a form of magick, the power of womanhood, of creation. I felt Alyce's deep ties to the earth, to the moon's cycles. I saw how strong women are, how much we can bear, how we can draw on the earth's deep power.

I felt a smile on my face, my eyes closed, joy welling up inside me. Alyce was me, and I was her, and we were together. It was beautiful magick, made more beautiful as I realized that as much as Alyce was sending toward me, she was also receiving from me. I saw her surprise, even her awe at my powers, the powers I was slowly discovering and becoming comfortable with. Eagerly she fed on my mind, and I was delighted by how exciting she found the breadth of my strength, the depth of my power, my magick that stretched back a thousand years within my clan. She shared my sorrow over Cal and rejoiced with me in the discovery of my love for Hunter. She saw all the questions I had about my birth parents, how I longed to have known them. Gladly I gave to her, opened myself to her thoughts, shared my heritage and my life

And it was in opening my mind to share with Alyce that I saw myself: saw how strong I could be if I realized my potential; saw the dangerously thin line between good and evil that I would walk my whole life; saw myself as a child, as I was now, as a woman in the future. My strength would be beautiful, awe-inspiring, if only I could find a way to make myself whole. I needed answers. Dimly I became aware of warm tears on my cheeks, their saltiness running into my mouth.

Slowly, gradually, we began to separate into two beings again, our one joined whole pulled into two, like mitosis. The separation was as jarring and uncomfortable as the joining had been, and I mourned the loss of Alyce in my consciousness and felt her mourn the loss of me. We pulled apart, our hands slipping from each other's shoulders. Then my spine straightened, and I frowned, my eyes snapping open.

I looked at Alyce and saw that she, too, was aware of a

third presence: there was Morgan, and Alyce, and some unnamed force that was intruding, reaching toward me, sending dark tendrils of influence into my mind.

"Selene," I gasped, and Alyce was already there, throwing up blocks against the dark magick that had crept around us like a bog wisp, like smoke, like a poisonous gas. The ward-evil spell came to me easily, remembered and retrieved, and without effort I said the words and drew the sigils and put up my own blocks against what I sensed coming toward me. Alyce and I knew each other, had each other's learning and essence, and I called on knowledge only minutes old to protect myself against Selene, scrying to find me, reaching out to control me.

She was gone in an instant.

When I opened my eyes again, the world had settled into relative normalcy: I was sitting on the wooden floor of Sky and Hunter's house, and they were kneeling close, outside the circles, watching us. Alyce was opposite me, opening her eyes and taking a deep breath.

"What was that?" Sky asked.

"Selene," I answered.

"Selene," Alyce said at the same time. "Looking for Morgan."

"Why would she need to look for me?" I asked.

"It's more getting in touch with your mind," Alyce explained. "Seeing where you are magickally. Even trying to control you from a great distance."

"But she's gone now, right?" said Hunter. When I nodded, he asked, "How did it go? How do you both feel?"

My eyes met Alyce's. I ran a mental inventory. "Uh, I feel strange," I said, and then I fainted.

13.
Charred

November 12, 1980

Another day, another fight with Daniel. His constant antagonism is exhausting. He hates Amyranth and everything about it, and of course he only knows a tiny, tiny part of it. If he knew anything like the whole story, he would leave me forever. Which is completely unacceptable. I've been trying to come to terms with this dilemma since I met him, and I still don't have an answer. He refuses to see the beauty of Amyranth's cause. I've rejected his attempts to show me the beauty of goody-two-shoes scholarship and boiling up garlic-and-ginger tisanes to help clear up coughs.

Why am I unable to let him go? No man has ever held this much sway over me, not even Patrick. I want to give Daniel up, I've tried, but I get only as far as wishing him gone before I start aching desperately to have him back. I *simply love him, want him. The irony of this doesn't escape me. When we're good together, we're really, truly good, and we both feel a joy, a completeness that can't be matched or denied. Lately, though, it seems like the good times are fewer and farther between—we have truly irreconcilable differences.*

If I bend Daniel's will to my own through magick, how much would he be diminished? How much would I?

—SB

When I woke up on Monday, I felt awful. I had dim memories of Hunter driving me home in Das Boot, with Sky following in her car. He had whispered some quick words in my ear on my front porch, and I was able to walk and talk and look halfway normal for my parents before I stumbled upstairs into bed with all my clothes on. How did I get out of the robe and back into my clothes? Ugh. I'd think about that later.

"Morgan?" Mary K. poked her head around the bathroom door. "You okay? It's almost ten o'clock."

"Mpf," I mumbled. Dagda, my gray kitten, padded in after her and leaped up onto my bedspread. He had grown so much in just a few weeks. Purring, he stomped his way up the comforter toward me, and I reached out to kiss his little triangular head and rub his ears. He collapsed, exhausted, and closed his eyes. I knew how he felt.

In fact, I knew how Mary K. felt as well. I opened my eyes again to see my sister regarding herself in the mirror. I could sense her feelings with more accuracy and immediacy than just sisterly intuition. Mary K. was sad and kind of lost. I frowned, wondering how I could help her. Then she turned around. "I guess I'll go over to Jaycee's. Maybe we can get her sister to take us to the mall. I've still got to get some Christmas presents."

"I'd take you," I said, "but I don't think I can get out of bed."

"Are you coming down with something?" she asked.

Not exactly, but . . . "Probably just a cold." I sniffled experimentally.

"Well, can I get you anything before I leave?"

I thought about food, and my stomach recoiled. "Do we have any ginger ale?"

"Yeah. You want some?"

"Sure."

I was able to keep the ginger ale down. I didn't feel sick, exactly, just drained and fuzzy. Other aftereffects of the brach were apparent as well. It was similar to what I'd felt after my first circle with Cal and Cirrus, but magnified by a factor of ten. My senses seemed even more heightened than they had that time: I could make out distinct threads in the jeans hanging over my desk chair; I saw tiny motes of dust caught in the new paint on my walls. Later in the morning I heard a bizarre crunching sound coming from downstairs, as if a hundred-pound termite was eating the basement. It turned out to be Dagda working on his kibble. I felt my lungs absorbing oxygen from every breath; felt my blood cells flowing through my veins, suspended in plasma; felt how each square inch of my skin interpreted and analyzed air or fabric or whatever touched it.

I felt magick everywhere, flowing around me, flowing out of me, in the air, in anything organic, in the sleeping trees outside, in Dagda, in anything that I touched.

I assumed this hyperawareness would fade gradually. It had better. It was wonderful, but if I were this sensitive all the time, I'd lose my mind.

A golden brownish maple leaf drifted past my window. It came to rest for an instant on the sill, and I gazed meditatively at it, marveling at the complex network of tiny veins that spread across its surface. I almost thought I could make out a face in the intersecting lines—a wide, firm mouth, straight nose, two golden eyes. . . .

Goddess. Cal.

In the next instant the leaf was caught in a gust of wind and danced away.

I lay there in bed, breathing deeply, trying to regain my lost peace. But it was hard, because although after yesterday I no longer feared Cal the way I had, every thought of Cal led to a thought of Selene and to the sure knowledge that she was still searching for me, still plotting to destroy me.

Gradually I became aware of something nagging at the edge of my consciousness. My quest. My search for more knowledge about my birth parents, my heritage. I hadn't done anything about it yet, but now, with the new clarity I had achieved as a result of the brach, I saw how much I needed to. Only then would I be whole; only then would my power be fully accessible to me; only then would it be truly mine. And only then would I have a hope against Selene.

Eventually I struggled to my feet and changed into clean clothes, dismissing a shower as unnecessary. I brushed my hair and my teeth and felt I'd done enough grooming for one day. After I flopped back onto my bed, I sensed Hunter coming up my front walk. I groaned, wanting to see him but knowing I could never make it downstairs to open the door.

"Hunter, just come in," I whispered, sending him a witch message.

Moments later I heard the front door snick open, then Hunter calling, "Morgan?"

"I'm upstairs," I managed to call. "You can come up." I wondered if I now had a spell in the recesses of my brain that would keep my mom from unexpectedly coming home from work.

His footsteps were light on the stairs, and then he was peering around my door. "Is it okay for me to be here?" he asked.

I smiled, pleased that he'd asked. "No one's here but me," I said.

"Right," said Hunter, coming in. "If we feel someone coming home, I'll jump out the window." He stood, tall and lean and newly familiar, and looked down at me. His hair was messy from his hat, and it stood up in pale gold spikes.

"Okay," I said. Cautiously I put out my senses and felt his awareness that I'd done so.

"How are you feeling?" he asked.

"Crappy. Weak. But really, really magicky." I couldn't help grinning.

He groaned theatrically. "Now I'm frightened. Please, please," he said. "I'm begging you. Please do not do anything with your new magick just yet. Do not cast spells. Do not run around town throwing witch fire at anyone. Promise me."

"It's like you don't trust my judgment or something," I said. He came to sit on the end of my bed and put one hand on my comforter-covered leg. I started to feel better.

"Oh," he said, rolling his eyes. "So you actually think you use judgment sometimes?"

I kicked him, and then we were grinning at each other, and I felt much better.

"That was an amazing brach last night," he said. "Very intense."

"It was," I agreed. "How's Alyce? Have you talked to her?"

He nodded. "Sky is with her, and another witch from Starlocket, too. She feels about like you do. She's excited, though. She got a lot from you."

"I got a lot from her," I said slowly. "I haven't begun to process it."

"It will take you a long time," Hunter predicted. Absently he rubbed my leg, below the knee, and I looked at his eyes, wondering how to say what I needed to.

"I'm so sorry about yesterday," I said, and his eyes darkened. I swallowed. "It was just—I couldn't go through that again. The last time—on the cliff—when I thought you were dead, that I had killed you. I just—couldn't go through that. I couldn't have you two fighting—trying to kill each other. Never again."

His face was still, watchful.

"I'm so sorry I put the binding spell on you," I said. "I know how horrible that feels. I've never forgiven Cal for doing it to me. Now I've done it to you. But I just didn't know how else to get out of there and to take you with me. I'm so sorry," I ended miserably.

"Cal needs to come in," Hunter said quietly. "He needs to answer to the council. And because of who I am and where I am, it will be me who has to bring him in."

I nodded, trying to accept that.

Hunter stroked my knee, and I felt a trembly sensation start at his fingertips and move up to the pit of my stomach. He was quiet for a long while, and I reached out and held his hand.

"Yule is tomorrow," he said finally.

"That's right. I lost track of the days. I hope I'll be up to celebrating by then."

"I think you will," he said with a smile.

"There's something else I need to do tomorrow," I said. "If I can move."

"What's that?"

"I need to go to Meshomah Falls." That was the town where my birth parents had briefly lived—and where they had died. "I want to find the place where the barn burned down."

"Why?" he asked.

"To learn," I said. "There's so much I don't know. Who set the fire? Why? I need to find out. I feel like I won't be whole until I do. That's what I learned from the brach."

Hunter looked at me for a long moment. "It's dangerous, you know," he said. "With Cal roaming about and Selene on her way."

I didn't say anything.

Then he nodded. "All right," he said. "I'll pick you up at ten, shall I?"

God, I loved him.

*   *   *

Hunter drove, because I was still a little shaky on Tuesday. He didn't bring up the subject of Cal, except to tell me that he still hadn't been able to locate him. "I wonder if he's got someone helping him," Hunter said, rubbing his chin, and I thought of Selene and felt a flash of dread. Was she here now? No. She couldn't be. I wasn't ready.

Then Hunter took my hand without speaking, and I felt his strength flowing into me, calming me. I am with you, he was saying without words. And I felt suddenly better, lighter.

I'd been to Meshomah Falls once before, and it felt familiar to me now. I directed Hunter to the outskirts of town. There was an old field there, tan and dry from the winter cold. I got out of the car and walked to the middle of it. I still felt weak, drained, as if I were getting over the flu.

Maeve's coven tools were in the trunk of the car, but I left them there. I didn't need them yet. Hunter came to stand next to me.

"Okay. Let's find the old barn site," he said.

I stood still, my arms slightly out by my sides, and shut down all thoughts, all feelings, all expectations. Soon I no longer felt the winter sun on my face or the wind in my hair. But I could see where the barn had been, see what it had looked like and what the site looked like now. I followed it in my mind, tracing how to get there from here. When it was clear, I opened my eyes, feeling vaguely nauseated.

"Okay, I got it," I said, and swallowed. I headed back to the car and the Diet Coke that was waiting there.

"Are you sure you're up to this?" Hunter asked as I swigged soda and held the cold can against my forehead.

"I have to do it," I said. "I just . . . I have to."

He nodded and started the car. "Yes, I think you're right. Tonight at the Yule circle we'll send you some restoring energy."

"Take the next left," I said, already feeling better.

We found it almost fifteen minutes later, after getting lost a couple of times. Like Widow's Vale, this area was hilly and rocky, the narrow roads lined with skeletal trees and bushes. In the springtime it would be beautiful and in the summer unbelievably lush and green. I hoped Maeve had found a small measure of happiness here, at least for a short while.

"There it is," I said, pointing suddenly. I recognized a twisted spruce as one that I'd seen in my mind's eye. "In there."

Hunter pulled the car to the side of the road and peered skeptically past the tree line. We got out, and I quickly jumped the old-fashioned slat fence. Hunter followed. I strode forward through the dead clumps of frozen grass, sending out my senses and looking alertly at everything. There was almost nothing alive around here, no birds, no animals hibernating in nests or trees, no deer or rabbits watching quietly nearby.

"Hmmm," said Hunter, slowing down and scanning the area. "What do you feel?"

I swallowed. "I feel like we're close to something really bad."

I slowed my pace and started looking more closely at the ground. Suddenly I halted, as if an invisible hand had pressed my chest and stopped me cold. I looked closer, focusing sharply on the ground between the clumps of grass. I didn't even know what to look for, but then I saw it: the rippled, broken backbone of a large brick foundation. The barn had once stood here.

I stepped back, as if it were poison ivy. Hunter came up next to me, looking uncomfortable and edgy.

"Now what?" he asked.

"I get my tools," I said.

I made Hunter turn around while I wiggled out of my clothes and put on Maeve's robe. No one but my mother, my sister, and my gynecologist had seen me naked, and I was going to keep it that way. At least for the immediately foreseeable future.

"Okay, I'm ready," I said, and Hunter turned to look at me.

"How do you want to do this?" he said. "I don't have my robe or tools with me."

"I'm thinking meditation," I answered. "Together, the two of us, with my tools."

Hunter thought about it and nodded. By picking our way through the years of overgrowth, we found two walls of the former foundation. Gauging our position from the angle of the crumbling bricks, we sat in what had been the center of the barn. I held Maeve's athame in my left hand, her wand in my right. Between Hunter and me I placed several crystals and two bloodstones. We drew a circle of power around us with a stick and then closed our eyes. I took a deep breath, tried to release tension, and lost myself in nothingness.

The inside of the barn was dark. Angus and I stood in the middle of the building, hearing running footsteps around the outside. I was muttering spells under my breath, spells I hadn't used in two years. My magick felt dull, blunted, an unhoned blade no longer useful. Beside me I felt Angus's fear, his hopelessness. Why are you wasting energy on feelings? I wanted to scream.

My eyes adjusted to the blackness inside the barn. The scents of old hay, animals from long ago, ancient leather filled my nose, and I wanted to sneeze. Still I chanted, drawing power to me:

"An di allaigh an di aigh . . ." I reached out with my senses, probing, but they recoiled on me. It was as if we were trapped in a cage made of crystal—a cage that reflected our power back at us rather than letting it out to do its work.

The first sharp scent of smoke came to me. Angus gripped my hand tightly, and I shook him off, feeling sudden anger at the way he'd loved me all these years—years when he'd known that I didn't love him. Why hadn't he demanded more from me? Why hadn't he left me? Then maybe he wouldn't be here now, dying with me.

Smoke. I heard the hungry crackling of the fire as it lapped the base of the barn, as it whipped down the sides, hurrying to meet itself, to make a full circle of flames. The barn was old, dry, the wood half rotted: perfect kindling. Ciaran had known.

"Our child." Angus's voice was full of pain.

"She's safe," I said, feeling guilt weighing on me, further weakening my powers. "She will always be safe." The small windows, high on the barn walls, glowed pinkly, and I knew it was from fire, not from dawn. No one would find us. Ciaran's magick would make sure of that. No one would call the fire department until it was much too late. Already the building was filling with smoke, hovering by the ceiling, swirling on itself, thickening.

Maybe it wasn't too late. Maybe I could find a way out. I still had my power, rusty though it might be. "An di allaigh an di aigh . . . ," I began once again.

But at my words, the cage of magick around us seemed to tighten, to contract, glittering as it pressed in on us. I coughed and inhaled smoke. And then I knew there was no hope.

It had come to this. Ciaran was going to be my death. He had shown me what love was, what it could be, and now he would show me my death. I felt sharp regret that Angus would die here, too. I tried to console myself with the fact that it had been his choice. He had always chosen to be with me.

I wondered what Ciaran was doing outside: if he was still watching, making sure we didn't escape; if he was weaving magick all around us, spells of death and binding, panic and fear. I felt panic's claws scraping at my mind, but I refused to let it in. I tried to keep calm, to call power to me. I thought about my baby, my beautiful baby, with her fine, fuzzy infant hair the color of my mother's. Her tilted, brown eyes, so like her father's. The most perfect baby ever born, with a thousand years of Belwicket magick in her veins, in her blood.

She would be safe from this kind of danger. Safe from her heritage. I had made sure of that.

It was hard to breathe, and I dropped to my knees. Angus was coughing, trying to breathe through his shirt, pulled up to cover his nose and mouth. I had mended that shirt this morning, sewed on a button.

Ciaran. Even here, now, I couldn't help remembering how he'd made me feel when we'd first met. It had been so clear we were meant to be together. So clear that we were muìrn beatha dàns. But he was married to another and a father. And I chose Angus. Poor Angus. Then Ciaran chose the darkness, over me.

I felt light-headed. Sweat was beading on my forehead, in my hair; soot was stinging my eyes. Angus was coughing nonstop. I took his hand as I sank into the fine dust on the barn floor, feeling the heat pressing in from all sides. I no longer chanted. It was no use. Ciaran had always been stronger than I—he had gone through the Great Trial.

I had never had a chance.

14.
Bait

November 1981

I'm pregnant. It's a bizarre physiological experience, like being taken over by an alien that I can't control. Every cell in my body is changing. It's thrilling and terrifying: much like being part of Amyranth.

Daniel, of course, is furious. These past six months he's always furious with me, so there's nothing new there. We'd agreed not to have children because our marriage has seemed so rocky. By myself, I decided I wanted to have part of Daniel always, wanted to have something permanent that was partly me and partly him. So I used magick to override his conception block. It was easy.

So Daniel's thrown a fit and hightailed it back to England. I've settled in San Francisco because of the strong Amyranth presence here. What is it about

England that pulls him back so strongly? This is the third time in three months that he's gone back. For me, my home is where Amyranth is. Daniel's sentimental loyalty seems naive and misplaced.

He'll be back soon. He always comes back. And the mirror shows me that pregnant, I am more beautiful than ever. When he sees me glowing, carrying our child, it will be a new start for us. I can feel it.

—SB

When I opened my eyes, tears were streaming down my face. Hunter was watching me, looking calm and alert. He reached toward me and brushed some tears away with his hand.

"Did you see any of that?" I asked, my throat tight and full of pain.

"Some," he said, helping me stand. We were both chilled through, and I wanted to be gone from this place, far away from these feelings. I looked down at the broken foundations and could still smell the ancient ash, the charred boards. I could hear the snap of the windows as they broke one by one from the heat. The smell of skin and hair, burning. They had been dead by then.

"The images I got were confused," said Hunter. He pulled me to him as we walked back to the car, and by the time I had changed out of my robe and was sitting in the passenger seat, I was crying hard, my hands over my face. Hunter hugged me, his arms around me, his hands stroking my hair.

"It was Ciaran," I finally got out. "The love of my mother's life. He killed her and Angus."

"Why?"

"I don't know," I said, frustrated. "Because he couldn't have her? Because she rejected him when she found out he was married? Because she chose Angus? I don't know."

I rested my head against Hunter's chest, feeling how lean and hard he was through his coat. I knew that he understood pain because of what had happened to his parents. Maybe someday, I'd be able to help Hunter as he was helping me now. Suddenly his fingers stilled against my back and tension entered his body. I raised my head and closed my eyes.

"Selene," I whispered, already throwing up the magick blocks I had learned from Alyce. I quickly erected wall after wall around me, sealing my mind off from outside influences, surrounding myself and Hunter with ward-evil spells, protection spells, spells of concealment and strength. It took only instants, and I felt Selene's increased pressure as she tried to get through, tried to get into my mind. My hand gripped Hunter's, and our powers joined—I felt his strength shoring up mine and was grateful.

Just like that, it was over. I no longer felt any other presence. Slowly Hunter and I let each other go, and I felt a pang of regret at losing that particular closeness.

"She wants you badly," Hunter said grimly, sitting back in his seat. "That's the second time she's tried to get into your mind. She must be closer than I thought. Dammit! We've searched everywhere for her—I scry every day. But I haven't been able to pick up on anything." He thought for a moment, drumming his fingers on the steering wheel. "I'm calling in help from the council." He started the car and turned on the heater.

"Will they really be able to help?" I asked, wrapping my arms around myself. I felt overwhelmed, sad and weary.

"I hope so," Hunter answered me. "Selene is working up to something, and it's going to happen soon. I feel it." He glanced over at me and put his hand on my leg. I was starting to thaw but still felt nauseated. I hoped I wouldn't have to ask Hunter to pull over so I could barf.

"Recline your seat," he suggested as I sipped the rest of my Diet Coke. "Are you sure you should be drinking that? We could stop and get a nice cup of tea somewhere."

"Coke settles your stomach," I said. "Everyone knows that." I put the can in the cup holder, then pulled the lever that reclined my seat.

"Better?" Hunter asked.

"Um," I said. My eyes felt heavy, and I let myself sink into a lovely lack of consciousness where there was no pain. The next thing I knew the car had stopped and Hunter was gently rubbing my shoulder.

"Home again, home again, jiggity jig," he said.

We were parked in front of my house. Through my window I saw that the day had turned ugly, with dark, heavy clouds rolling in from the west. It looked like snow was on the way. My watch said it was four o'clock.

I reached for the handle to straighten my seat but was caught by the expression in Hunter's eyes. All at once he seemed like the most beautiful thing I had ever seen, and I smiled at him. His eyes flared slightly, and he leaned down. I curled my arms around his neck and held him to me as our mouths met. Eagerly I kissed him, wanting to join with him, wanting to show him how I felt about him, how much I appreciated him. His breathing quickened as he held me closer, and it was thrilling to know how much he wanted me, too.

Slowly he pulled back, and our breathing gradually returned to normal.

"We need to talk about what you saw," he said quietly, stroking one finger along my jaw.

I nodded. "Maybe you could come in for a while? We could hang out in the den. My mom will more or less leave us alone in there."

He grinned at me, and we walked up to my front door. Before I could unlock it, it opened, and my mom looked at me kind of wild-eyed.

"Morgan! Thank goodness you're home! Do you know where Mary K. is? Is she with you?" She looked past me as if expecting to see my sister walking up the driveway.

"No," I answered, feeling a jolt of alarm. "I saw her this morning. She said she was going to Jaycee's."

"They haven't seen her all day," my mom said, the lines around her mouth deepening. "I came home early, and there was a message from Jaycee asking why Mary K. had stood her up."

Mom stepped aside and motioned us to come in. I was thinking about possibilities, my brain firing fast, battling the weariness I'd had since Sunday.

"Did she leave a note? What does her room look like?" I asked.

"No note anywhere, and her room is fine, like she just left," said my mom. "Her bicycle is here." Her voice sounded strained. I knew what she was thinking: Bakker.

"Let me call Bakker's house," I said, shrugging out of my coat. I headed for the kitchen, looked up Bakker's number, and dialed it. Maybe his family would know where he had gone. Maybe Mary K., using incredibly bad judgment, was there watching TV or something.

His mother answered, and I asked to speak to Bakker. To my relief, he was home, and soon said a cautious, "Hello?"

"Bakker, it's Morgan Rowlands," I said briskly. "Where's Mary K.?"

"Huh?" he said, instantly defensive. "How would I know?"

"Look, is she there? Just let me talk to her."

"Are you kidding? Thanks to you, she'll never speak to me again. I haven't seen her since school let out."

"It's *your* fault she won't speak to you," I said scathingly. "If I find out she's there and you're lying to me—"

"She's not here. Go screw yourself." Click.

I looked up to see Mom and Hunter watching me. "Apparently she's not with Bakker," I said. I tapped my finger against my lips, thinking. Mary K. had been so different lately. She'd been going to church so often, praying and reading the Bible. I felt a pang of guilt, thinking of all the times I'd tried to talk to her but hadn't pushed her to open up to me. She might be in real trouble now, and maybe I could have prevented it.

"Maybe she just went shopping or something," I said, not believing it. "Or maybe she went to an afternoon service at church. But why would she stand up Jaycee?"

"She wouldn't," said Mom, and I felt her tension, felt how close she was to panicking. "She would never do that. You know how conscientious she is."

I looked at Hunter and saw that he was thinking the

same thing I was: that we should scry to find Mary K., and that we couldn't do it in front of my mom.

"Okay," I said, reaching for my coat. "Tell you what. Hunter and I will go and look at the coffee shop and church, maybe Darcy's house, and some of the shops downtown. We'll call you in an hour with an update, but I'm sure we'll find her. She probably just forgot to leave a note. I'm sure she's okay, and there's a simple explanation."

"Okay," my mom said after a moment. "I'm probably over-reacting. It's just so unlike her to take off like this." She bit her lip. "I already called Dad. He's on his way home. He said he'd take a look around the Taunton mall, see if she's there."

"It'll be okay. We'll call you." Hunter and I went out the front door and started down the walk toward his car. I felt like I'd been in that car all day and didn't want to get back in it. Just as we reached the sidewalk, our next-door neighbor, Mrs. DiNapoli, walked over from her house.

"Hi, Morgan," she said, drawing her coat around her. "Is your mother home?" She smiled and held out a glass meas-uring cup. "I need to borrow—"

"Sugar?" I asked.

"Flour," she said. "Harry's aunt and uncle are coming to dinner, and I'm making a roux. Do you think your folks have any flour?"

"Um, probably," I said as Hunter smiled at Mrs. DiNapoli and opened the driver's side door. "Mom's inside—you can ask her. We were just on our way out."

"Okay." She headed up our driveway as I turned to get in. "That was some car earlier," Mrs. DiNapoli called back. "Whose was it?"

"What do you mean?" I asked.

"That Jaguar Mary K. got into earlier."

I froze. "You saw Mary K. getting into a Jaguar?" I'm so stupid, I thought. Why didn't I ask any of the neighbors if they had seen anything?

Mrs. DiNapoli laughed. "Yes, a beautiful green one."

Selene drove a green Jaguar. I looked at Hunter, and again our thoughts were in accord. He nodded at me briefly, then slid behind the wheel and started the engine.

"I'm not sure whose it was," I said. "How long ago was this?"

Our neighbor shrugged. "Two hours, at least. I'm not sure."

"Okay, thanks, Mrs. DiNapoli." I climbed into the passenger seat and Hunter took off, heading out of town. We knew where we needed to start looking.

Cal's old house.

15.
Trap

April 1982

Be careful what you wish for, they say. Because you may get it.

I've gotten what I wished for, and the Goddess must be laughing. Daniel's come home, after being gone almost three months. The baby is due in June, and I look big and vibrant and fertile, like the Goddess herself. It's been interesting to see how pregnancy affects my magick: I'm more powerful in some ways, but there are some unpredictable side effects. Some spells fall apart, some have unexpected results. Nothing can be counted on. It's funny, for the most part. However, for the last seven months I've haven't been able to do my part for Amyranth. They've been understanding, though—they know I'll soon present them with a perfect Amyranth baby, one literally born to do their work.

It's hard for me to put the next words down. I've found out the reason Daniel goes to England so much: he has a girl-friend there. He actually told me this himself. I was sure he was joking—what woman, witch or human, can compete with me? But as he droned on and the words started sinking in, I went through being amused, then horrified, then furious. This other woman, whom he won't name, and he have known each other for years and had a childhood romance. But their affair only started six months ago—right after I conceived my baby. I'm shocked beyond words. The idea that Daniel could keep such a secret from me is unbelievable. It means his powers are stronger than I knew, and how is that possible?

I'm thinking about what to do next. That this other woman has to be found and eliminated goes without saying. Daniel says their affair is over. Pathetically, he wept when he told me. What a worm! He came back to me for the sake of the baby we're having, but he won't sleep with me and says he won't pretend we're a couple anymore. This won't do at all. He's going to be mine or no one's. I have to break his will, bind him to me. Now I must go—I have research to do and people to consult.

—SB

Hunter pulled over while we were still a mile from Cal's. He cut the engine and turned to me.

"Why are you stopping?" I said urgently. "Let's go! If she has Mary K.—"

"I know, and we'll get there. But first, send Sky and Alyce a witch message," he said. "I'd send it, but yours will be stronger. Tell them to contact the council and get reinforcements to Selene's as fast as they can. It will take a couple of hours at least, but maybe they can get here in time to help us."

"Should I ask Sky and Alyce to meet us there now?" I asked. "We could all join our powers. . . ."

He shook his head. "They aren't equipped for this battle," he said gently. "Neither are you, if it comes to that. But this is about you, about what Selene wants from you."

"I'll be strong enough," I said, not at all sure that was true. "If she's done anything to Mary K.—"

"What's important is that you use your own powers," Hunter said, looking at me intently. "Use your powers, coupled with Alyce's knowledge. Feel the power within you. Know it absolutely. Selene is going to try to use illusion and fear to break you down. Don't let it work."

I looked into his eyes, feeling dread. "All right," I said shakily.

He started the engine. Five minutes later he was turning down the street that led to the huge stone house where Cal and Selene had worked their magick.

Darkness was all around us. It was barely five o'clock but wintertime, and the sun had sunk below the horizon, obscured by ominous-looking clouds. I could feel that soon the sky would open and start dumping snow and ice.

Mary K., I thought as Hunter parked down the street, out of sight of the big house. My sweet sister. Although we shared no blood, I felt we had always been sisters in spirit: destined to be related to each other, to love each other as family. In some ways she was so much savvier than I—she knew what to wear, who to hang out with, how to flirt and be cheerful and charming. But in some ways she was so naive. She trusted most people. She believed that her faith would protect her. She believed that if she was good enough, everything would work out. I knew better than that.

"Pop the trunk," I told Hunter, and he did. I knew I would need every ounce of power I could possibly have: I was still feeling the draining effects of the tàth meànma brach. Without more than a moment's awkward hesitation I stripped off my coat, sweatshirt, and undershirt and put on my mother's robe, the thin emerald green silk instantly warming me in the cold night air. I felt my cheeks heat with a blush as I unsnapped my jeans and pushed them and my underwear down. Of course then I realized I still wore my sneaks and socks and had to kneel and get out of them to get out of my pants.

Then I stood, feeling completely comfortable in the robe and nothing else even though it was winter in upstate New York. Like a Wiccan force field, I thought, picking up Maeve's wand and athame.

"I wish I'd had time to collect my own robe," Hunter said, frowning. He pulled out his athame. Thus armed, we began to move quietly toward the house.

We were immediately aware of a darkness of magick all around. Keeping to the shadows of the hedge that surrounded the property, I cast out my senses and felt a miasma of black magick emanating from the house, from the stones themselves. The green Jaguar sat in the circular driveway, and to my eyes it seemed to glow and pulse, almost as if it were radioactive. I realized that I was terrified and tried to release my fears.

In unspoken agreement we paused, and together we wrapped ourselves in cloaks of illusion, of vagueness, of shadows. With no effort I pulled spells out of Alyce's memory and called them to me, as familiar to me as Dagda. Under any other circumstances I would have felt thrilled with my new ability, but now I merely fretted. To any lesser witch we would certainly be undetectable, but would these spells work on Selene? She was so powerful that I doubted it.

We looked at the house, with its gaping black windows, its air of recent neglect. Dried leaves had blown onto the porch and steps and remained unswept.

"How did she get in?" I whispered. "The house was spelled against her."

"The council did its best," Hunter replied softly. "But Selene has powers and connections we don't fully understand. The question is, how can *we* get in? The front door will be a trap."

I crouched down for a moment, examining the house. Then an idea came to me, and I stood up. "Come with me."

Without waiting for his response, I strode along the hedge until we reached a break in the tall shrubbery to the right of the house. We crunched across dead grass, around to the back, where a narrow metal staircase led up to the third-floor attic. Cal's old room. I started climbing, my bare feet making hardly any sound.

"We spelled all the entrances," Hunter reminded me quietly.

"I know. But you can break your spells; you made them. And I don't think Selene will expect us to come in this way." The whole time I climbed, I was feeling with my senses, searching for my sister, for Selene's presence, trying to get through the spells of privacy that cloaked the house. I could feel nothing except an aching, bone-deep weariness, the faint edges of nausea around the rim of my consciousness, and the seeping of tendrils of dark magick writhing in the air all around me.

At the top of the narrow staircase was a small wooden door. Cal used to use it to get from his room to the backyard and to the pool beyond. I stopped for a moment, pressed my hand against my brow, closed my eyes, and concentrated.

It wasn't as if everything suddenly popped out at me in neon colors. But as I thought, willing magick to show itself to me, the layers of the spells on the door slowly and faintly began to glimmer. I was vaguely aware of Hunter, next to me, becoming very still and alert as the sigils and markings of spells shone with a slight sheen around the door frame. I saw the oldest markings, those of Cal himself, spelling the door so that it would open only to his command. I can't say how I knew these spells were his, how I knew what they were and how he had made them. It was more like seeing a daisy and thinking, Daisy. It was clear and instantaneous.

It was also clear that Cal's spells had been mostly obliterated, I guessed by the International Council of Witches. Their spells were complicated and gleamed brightly. I didn't know the council members well enough to recognize their handiwork but felt that I saw traces of Hunter's handwriting, his personality in the spells. Again I could never have explained it or proved it. I just knew.

Overlying everything were dark, spiky spells of illusion and repulsion that I recognized as Selene's handiwork. She had used an ancient alphabet and an archaic set of characters, and just seeing the spells written there brought forth a wave of fear that I tried to dismiss. Selene's work glowed the brightest: she had cast these spells recently.

"All right," breathed Hunter next to me. I kept the spells in sight as he began slowly and laboriously dismantling them, layer by layer, saying the words that unknit the spells, dispersing their energy and power. My head was beginning to ache with a sharp, piercing pain at my temples as I strove to concentrate. The cold wind seemed to intensify, and it buffeted us as we stood on that narrow staircase outside the attic of the stone house.

At last the spells were taken apart, and then it was simple for Hunter to magickally undo the mechanical lock of the door. It swung open silently, and with a glance at each other, Hunter and I stepped through.

Inside, Cal's room was as he'd left it that night he'd tried to kill me. With a quick scan I saw he had taken some of his books, and probably some clothes, since his dresser drawers were pulled askew. But it didn't appear that he'd been staying here.

The room was startlingly familiar, and it brought an unwelcome ache to my heart to see the place where Cirrus had had circles, the chair where I'd opened my birthday presents from Cal, the bed where we had lain and kissed for hours.

As noiselessly as possible, we did a quick search of Cal's room. I held my athame before me and on virtually every surface turned up runes, sigils, other markings: the magick Cal had worked in this room. But other than the marks, and some dangerous tools and talismans, we found nothing, no sign of Mary K. or of Cal's or Selene's whereabouts.

"This way," Hunter said, his voice no louder than a whisper, and motioned toward the door that led to the rest of the house. When he opened the door, I almost recoiled. Now I could sense Selene, feel her dark presence. She had been working black magick in this house: its bitter and acrid aura clung to everything. It felt like the very air was contaminated, and I was afraid.

Gently Hunter brushed his hand against my hair, my cheek. "Remember," he whispered. "Fear is one of her weapons. Don't give in to it. Trust your instincts."

My instincts? I thought, panicked. We both knew how reliable *those* had been in the past. But I knew that was the wrong answer, so I just nodded, and we started down the narrow back staircase to the second floor. Maeve's wand felt slim and powerful in my left hand, and the athame felt as protective as a shield. But I still felt vulnerable as I crept downstairs and was glad Hunter was beside me.

Cal's room took up the entire attic, and on the second floor were five bedrooms and four bathrooms. Here, as upstairs, the dusty floors were undisturbed until our feet traced patterns on them. To a rational mind, that meant that no person had walked here since the house had been shut. But witchcraft is not bound by laws of rationality.

Searching as a witch was different than searching as a person. I used my eyes and ears, but more important, I used my senses, my intuition, my Wiccan instinct that warned me when danger was near and what form it would take. Between me, my tools, and Hunter, we made short work of the second floor. None of the rooms looked touched, but more telling, none of the rooms *felt* touched. I didn't detect

Selene's unmistakable aura in any of the bedrooms: she hadn't been to the second floor.

The only time I felt anything at all was when I paused before an open window in the last bedroom. I felt a faint chill there, as if I stood beneath an AC vent, but the window curtains were motionless, and then I picked up on it: Cal. Cal had been here; he'd stood here with a lit candle not long ago. The day Bree, Mary K., and I had come back from Practical Magick and I had seen him. His traces lingered here still.

Hunter came to stand by me. Our eyes met, and he nodded. He felt it, too. Taking my elbow, he led me to the main staircase, the wide, ornately carved steps leading to the first floor. The rich carpet looked dull, dusty, and my nose tickled as our feet stirred motes into the chill, silent air.

Selene's presence felt stronger with every step. In my hand, the hilt of the ancient Belwicket athame seemed to grow warm. Then I knew: Selene was in her library, the hidden library that I had seen only once, a lifetime ago, when I had discovered Maeve's Book of Shadows on Selene's shelves. When Hunter had come here, he hadn't even been able to find the concealed door. In fact, the council witches themselves hadn't been able to break the spells that guarded Selene's secret lair.

Today would be different. Today we would get into the hidden library because today Selene wanted us to. She had taken my sister to try to make me come here. In an instant I saw the whole plan: Selene had been trying to get into my mind and had been thwarted by my ability to block her. Had she then turned to my sister? Mary K. had been withdrawn and sad for weeks—was Selene working on her mind even then?

Since she had first met me, Selene had been courting me, through her son. She had commanded Cal to get close to me, and he had. She had wanted him to make me love him, and he had. She had wanted him to convince me to join their side, to ally my magick and Maeve's coven tools with theirs. This I had refused. Since then she had wanted two things: my compliance or death and Maeve's tools. And now here I was, in her house, at her bidding, just as she had planned.

Today we would finish what had been set in motion the day we met. With a sudden, chilling certainty I knew that Selene intended for only one of us to survive this encounter: her. By the end of the day she wanted me dead and she wanted Maeve's tools. No doubt she also wanted Hunter dead. Mary K. probably didn't matter much to her, but as a witness, she would have to die as well.

I almost sagged against the stair rail as these thoughts flashed like lightning across my mind. If I were a full, initiated witch, I would be quaking in my boots at the idea of facing Selene Belltower. If I had the entire council standing behind me, wands raised, I would still feel a cold and desperate terror. As it was, there was only me and Hunter, and I was just a barefoot, talented amateur from a small town.

I gulped and looked at Hunter, my eyes wide and filling with hopeless tears. Jesus, get me out of this, I thought in panic. Please, God. Hunter watched me, his eyes narrowed, and then he reached out and gripped my shoulder hard, so hard, I winced. "Don't be afraid," he whispered fiercely.

Yeah, right, I wanted to scream. Every cell in my body wanted to turn, run, and get the hell out of here. Only the image of my innocent sister, trustingly getting into Selene's car, kept me in place. I felt nausea rise in the back of my throat, and I wanted to sit down and start crying, right there on the steps.

"Morgan, come." Selene's voice spoke in my mind.

My eyes widened, and I looked at Hunter. His face showed me that he hadn't heard it.

"Selene," I whispered. "She knows I'm here."

Hunter's face hardened. Leaning over, he put his mouth close to mine. "We can do this, love. You can do this."

I tried to focus, but I couldn't stop thinking that I might die today. A deep despair started in the pit of my stomach, as if I had swallowed a cold stone the size of my fist.

But there was nothing to be done. Mary K. was here. She was my sister, and she needed me now. Hunter was by my side as I took a step downward, my bare feet making no sound on the thick carpet. When we reached the bottom of the steps, the parquet floor was cold and dust covered. Here, at last, were signs of disturbance. I saw dim outlines of footprints, swept mostly away by something soft and heavy— the bottom of a cape? A blanket?

I turned and headed down the hallway toward the large kitchen. Halfway down the hall I stopped and looked to my right. The door had to be around here somewhere, I knew. The door to Selene's library.

16.
Selene

June 1982

Praise the Goddess. I finally had my baby boy. He is a big, perfect baby, with fine dark hair like mine and odd, slate-colored eyes that will no doubt change color later. Norris Hathaway and Helen Ford attended as midwives and were absolute lifesavers during labor. Labor! Goddess, I had no idea. I felt I was being rent in two, torn apart, giving birth to an entire world. I tried to be strong but I admit I screamed and cried. Then my son crowned, and Norris reached down to twist out his shoulders. I looked down to see my son emerge into the light, and my tears of pain turned to tears of joy. It was the most incredible magick I've ever made.

His naming ceremony will be next week. I've decided on Calhoun: warrior. His Amyranth name is Sgàth, which means darkness. It's a sweet darkness, like his hair.

Daniel didn't come to the birth: a sign of his weakness. He slouches around, mooning over England and his whore there, which makes me despise him, though I can't stop wanting him. He seems pleased with his son, less pleased with me. Now that our baby is here, flesh and blood, beautiful and perfect, perhaps Daniel will find happiness with me. It would be best for him if he did.

Now that I've had the baby, I'm hungry to get back to work with Amyranth. They were in Wales and then in Germany in the past several months, and I was gnashing my teeth with envy. The Germany trip yielded some ancient books on darkness that I can't wait to see—I can already taste them. It will be intensely fulfilling for me to watch Calhoun grow up within the arms of Amyranth, their son as well as mine. He will be my instrument, my weapon.

—SB

Selene wasn't going to make it *too* easy: it took Hunter and me several minutes to even find the dim outlines of the concealed door. Finally I managed to come up with one of Alyce's revealing spells and, using my athame, detected the barest fingernail-thin line in the hallway wall.

"Ah," Hunter breathed. "Well done."

I stood by, concentrating, lending my power to Hunter while he carefully, slowly, and methodically dismantled the concealment and closure spells. I felt Selene's magick as bursts of pain that needled into every part of my body, but I thought about Mary K., and I tried to ignore them.

It felt like hours later that Hunter passed his hand down the wall and I heard the faint snick of the latch opening. The door, barely taller than Hunter's head, swung open.

The next instant I clamped my mouth shut as darkness and evil surged through the doorway like a flood tide, coming to suck us under and into the room. Instinctively I stepped back, throwing up ward-evil spells and spells of protection on top of the ones Hunter and I had already placed on ourselves. Then I heard the soft, dark velvet of Selene's laughter, from inside the library, and I forced myself to take a step forward, across the threshold, into her lair.

It was dark in the room. The only light present was coming from several black pillar candles on wrought-iron holders taller than me. I remembered the layout from the only other time I had been here: it was a big room, with a high ceiling. Bookshelves lined the walls, connected by brass railings and small ladders on wheels. There was a deep leather couch, several glass display cases, Selene's huge walnut desk, a library table with a globe, and several book stands holding enormous, ancient, crumbling tomes. And everywhere in the room, in every book and cushion and rug, was Selene's magick, her dark magick, her forbidden spells and experiments and concoctions. The needlelike pains intensified as I scanned the room for Mary K.

Hunter moved behind me, coming into the room. I sensed danger coming from him, a deep, controlled anger at Selene's obvious misuse of magick.

"Morgan!" Mary K.'s soft, young voice came from a dark corner of the room. I cast out my senses and detected my sister huddled against the far wall. Sweeping the room for signs of Selene, I walked quickly to Mary K. and knelt down beside her.

"Are you okay?" I murmured, and she leaned forward, pressing her face against me.

"I don't know why I'm here," she said. Her voice was thick, as if she'd just woken from a deep sleep. "I don't know what's going on."

I was ashamed to tell her she had been merely bait, intended to lure me here. I was ashamed to admit that she was in terrible danger because of me and my Wiccan heritage. Instead I said, "It'll be okay. We'll get you out of here. Just hold on, okay?"

She nodded and slumped back down. Just in touching her I had felt that she was spelled—not strongly, but enough to make her lax and docile. Rage sparked deep in my stomach, and I stood. Hunter was still close to the door, and I saw he had prudently wedged a small wooden trunk in its opening.

Where was Selene? I'd heard her laugh. Of course, it could have been an illusion, a glamor. I was panicking: would I be locked in and trapped here? Would Selene set me on fire? Would I burn to death after all? My breathing quickened, and I peered into the darkest shadows of the room.

"Selene will try to scare you," Hunter had said. "Don't be fooled." Easier said than done. I stepped closer to one of the pillar candles and focused on it. Light, I thought. Fire. There were candles in holders on the walls, and around the room were candelabras filled with tall black tapers. One by one I lit them with my mind, sparking them into life, into existence, and the shadows lessened and the room grew brighter.

"Very good," said Selene's voice. "But then, you're a fire fairy. Like Bradhadair."

Bradhadair had been Maeve's Wiccan name, the name given her by her coven. It had been in her Book of Shadows, and probably no one else alive today knew about it. I swung toward the sound of Selene's voice and saw her appear in front of one of the bookcases, stepping out from a deep shadow into the light. She was as beautiful as ever, with her sun-streaked dark hair and strange golden eyes, so like Cal's. This was his mother. She had made him what he was.

Like me, Selene wore only her witch's robe, which was a deep crimson silk embroidered all over with symbols I recognized as the same ancient alphabet she'd used for the door spell. It had been taught to Alyce only so she could recognize it and neutralize it: it was inherently evil, and the letters could only be used for dark magick. Because Alyce had learned it, I knew it, too.

"Morgan, thank you for coming," Selene said. Out of the corner of my eye I saw Hunter circling the room, trying to put Selene between me and him. "I'm truly sorry I had to resort to these means. I assure you I've caused no harm to your sister. But once I realized you wouldn't respond to an ordinary invitation, well, I had to get creative." She gave me a charming, rueful smile and seemed like the most attractive person I'd ever seen. "Please forgive me."

I regarded her. Once I had admired her intensely, envied her knowledge and power and skill. Now I knew better.

"No," I said clearly, and her eyes narrowed.

"It's over, Selene," Hunter said in a voice like ice. "You've had a long run, but your days with Amyranth are done."

Amyranth? What's that? I wondered.

"Morgan?" Selene asked, ignoring Hunter.

"No," I repeated. "I don't forgive you."

"You don't understand," she said patiently. "You don't know enough to realize what you're doing. Hunter here is simply weak and misguided, and who cares? He isn't worth anything to anyone. But you, my dear. You have potential I can't ignore." She smiled again, but it was creepy this time, like a skeleton baring its teeth. "I offer you the chance to be more powerful than you could possibly imagine," she went on. I could hear the sibilant swish of her robe as she moved closer to me. "You are one of the few witches I've met who's worthy of being one of us. You could add to our greatness instead of draining us. You—and your coven tools."

My fists instinctively tightened on my wand and athame, and I tried to release the tension in my body. I had to stay loose and calm, to let the magick flow.

"No," I said again, and my senses picked up the instantaneous flare of anger from Selene. She quickly clamped it down, but the fact that I even felt it meant she wasn't as much in control of herself as she needed to be. I took a deep breath and went against every instinct that I had: I tried to relax, to open myself up, to stop protecting myself. I released anger, fear, distrust, my desire for revenge: I kept thinking, Magick is openness, trust, love. Magick is beauty. Magick is strength and forgiveness. I am made of magick. I thought how I felt after my tàth meànma brach, how I felt that magick was everywhere, in everything, in every molecule. If magick surrounded me, it was mine for the taking. I could access it. I could use it. I had the power of the world at my fingertips if I chose to let it in.

I chose to.

The next moment found me doubled over, gasping, as a wave of searing, biting pain hit me. I gagged, choking on the horrible cramping agony, and then I was on my hands and knees on the floor, sucking in breath and feeling like I was being turned inside out.

"Morgan!" Hunter said, but I was only barely aware of him. Every nerve in my body was being flayed, every sense I had was occupied with the exquisite, soul-consuming torture. My hands, still gripping the tools, clawed into the carpet as an invisible ax cleaved my belly in two. In disbelief I stared at myself, expecting to see guts and blood spewing from my body, but I was whole, unchanged on the outside. And yet I was gasping, writhing on the ground as my insides were eaten by acid.

It was an illusion. I knew it intellectually. But my body didn't know it. Between spasms I glanced up at Selene. She was smiling, a small, secret smile that showed me she enjoyed causing me agony.

"Morgan, you're stronger than that!" Hunter snapped, and his words seeped into my consciousness. "Get up! She can't do this to you!"

She's a playground bully, I thought, my breath coming in fast, shallow pants. When I had bound Cal and Hunter, had knocked them to the ground, I had felt the dark, shameful pleasure of controlling another person. That's what Selene was feeling now.

It was an illusion. Everything in me thought I was dying. But I was more than just my thoughts, more than just my feelings, more than my body. I was Morgan of Kithic and of Belwicket, and I had a thousand years of Woodbane strength inside me.

I feel no pain, I thought. I feel no panic.

Slowly I rose back up to my hands and knees, my mouth parched, sweat popping out on my forehead. My hair dragged on the ground, my hands were claws around my tools. *My* tools. They were not Maeve's. Not any longer.

I feel no pain, I thought fiercely. I am fine. Everything in my life is perfect, whole, and complete. I am strength. I am power. I am magick.

Then I was standing tall, my back straight, my hands at my sides. I looked calmly at Selene and for one fraction of a second saw disbelief in her eyes. More than disbelief. I saw the barest hint of fear.

Whirling, she turned to face Hunter and threw out her hand. I saw no witch fire, but Hunter immediately raised his hands and drew sigils in the air. His chest heaved as he pulled in breath, and though I couldn't actually see anything, I knew that Selene was trying to do to him what she had done to me and that he was resisting it. I had never seen so much of his power, not even when he was putting the braigh on David Redstone, and it was awesome.

But it wasn't enough for us to resist Selene. We had to actually vanquish her. We had to render her powerless somehow. I searched Alyce's data banks, concealed within my brain, and began to sift through the encyclopedias of knowledge she had acquired in her lifetime.

How do you fight darkness with light? I asked myself. In the same way that sunlight dispels a shadow, came the unhelpful answer. I almost screamed with frustration—I needed something practical, something concrete. Not mumbo jumbo.

The edge of my senses picked up a slight breathing

sound—Mary K. She sat, as motionless as a doll, her open eyes unseeing, in the shadows of the corner. Without thinking, I quickly called up spells of distraction, of turn-away. If Selene looked at Mary K., I wanted her to shift focus slightly, to see nothing, to not remember my sister's presence.

Hunter and Selene were facing each other, and suddenly Hunter surprised me by snatching up a crystal globe from a shelf and humming it at Selene. Her eyes widened and she stepped sideways, but the globe hit her shoulder with an audible thunk. In the next instant she flung out her hand and an athame flew across the room, straight at Hunter. It reminded me too much of that awful night weeks ago, and I flinched, but Hunter deflected the knife easily, and it glanced off a lamp and fell to the ground.

What could I do? I had no experience at things whizzing through the air—I had never practiced controlling physical things like that. In this battle I would need to use magick and magick alone. I would need to use my truth.

I saw Hunter pull out his braigh, the silver chain that was spelled to prevent its wearer from making magick. Coupled with some spells, it was enough to stop most witches.

But Selene merely glanced at Hunter with contempt, dismissing his threat and turning to me. Walking quickly across the room, she said, "Morgan, stop this foolishness. Call off your watchdog. You have it in you to be one of the greatest witches of all time: you are a true Woodbane, pure and ancient. Don't deny your heritage any longer. Join us, my dear."

"No, Selene," I said. Inside me, I consciously opened the door to my magick and with a deep, indrawn breath allowed it to flow. The first strains of a power chant began to thread their way into my mind.

Her beautiful face hardened, and I once again realized what I was up against. Hunter had said that Selene had been wanted by the council for years—that she had been implicated in countless deaths. Clinging to calmness, I nevertheless wished every member of the council would suddenly burst through the open door, capes waving, wands brandished, spells spouting from their lips. Coming here alone had been desperate. It had been crazy. Worse, it had been stupid.

Hunter began moving on Selene. His lips were moving, his eyes intent, and I knew he was starting the binding spells he used as a Seeker. Seeming bored, Selene barely waved a hand at him, and he stopped still, blinking. Then he started forward again, and again she stopped him.

With my mind I reached out, closed my eyes, and tried to see what I felt was there. I saw that Selene was putting up blocks and that Hunter was working through the blocks— but not as quickly as she was able to put them up. I also saw the first thin ribbons of my power spell coming to me, floating toward me on the winds of my heritage. I reached out for them, but Selene interrupted me.

"Morgan, don't you want to know the truth about how your mother died?"

17.
Shift

Yule, 1982

The house is decorated with yew boughs and holly, wintergreen and mistletoe. Red candles burn and catch Cal's eyes, now golden, like mine. This is his first Yule, and he loves it.

I found out that Daniel's whore in England had a baby, a boy, a month ago. It's Daniel's. She named him Giomanach. Daniel must be shielding her, because I haven't been able to find her, this Fiona, and get rid of her. Now I'm going to ask Amyranth to help me. It's hard to describe the feelings I have. It's so painful to admit to humiliation, despair, fury. If I were truly strong, I would strike Daniel dead. In my fantasies I've done that a thousand times—I've put his head on a spike in my front yard, cut out his heart, and mailed it to dear Fiona. I would *cry* to see her opening the box, seeing his heart. I would laugh.

Except that this is Daniel. I don't understand why I feel about him the way I do. Goddess help me, I can't stop loving him. If my love for him could be cut out from me, I would take up an athame and do it. If my need for him could be burned out, I would sear myself with witch fire or candle fire or an athame heated red hot in flame.

The fact that I still love him, despite his betrayal, despite the fact that he had a bastard with another woman, is like a sickness. I asked him how it had happened: were they both such poor witches that they couldn't even weave a contraceptive spell? He snapped at me and said no, the child was an accident, conceived of honest emotion. Unlike Calhoun, who had been my decision alone. He stormed out, into the wet San Francisco fog. He'll be back. It'll be against his will, but he always returns.

The joy in my life right now consists of one being, one perfection who delights me. Cal at six months is surpassing all my hopes and expectations. He has wisdom in his baby eyes, a hunger for knowledge I recognize. He's a beautiful child and easy: calm tempered yet determined, willful yet heartbreakingly sweet. To see his face light up when I come in makes everything else worthwhile. So this Yule is a time of darkness and light, for me as well as the Goddess.

—SB

I blinked and snapped my head to look at Selene. She will use anything against you, I thought. Even your dead mother. This is why you needed to know yourself. And you do.

At once Selene seemed pathetic, like an ant, like an insect, and I felt all-powerful. In my mind the ancient ribbons of power, the crystalline tune that contained the true name of magick itself, intensified.

"I know exactly how my mother died," I answered evenly, and saw her flicker of surprise. "She and Angus were burned to death by Ciaran, her mùirn beatha dàn."

I felt rather than saw Selene sending out fast, dark tendrils of magick, and before they reached me, I put up a block around myself so I remained untouched inside it, free of her anger. I felt the urge to laugh at how easy it was.

But Selene was older than I, much more educated than I, and in the end she knew how to fight better than I did. "You're seeing only what Hunter wants you to see," she said with a frightening intensity. She moved closer to me still, her eyes glowing like a tiger's, lit from within. "He has been controlling you these past weeks. Can't you see that? Look at him."

For some stupid reason I actually did flick a glance toward Hunter. "Don't listen to her!" he gasped, walking toward me with halting movements.

Before my eyes, the Hunter I had come to know changed: the bones of his face grew heavier, his jaw sharper, his mouth more cruel. His eyes sank into shadow. His skin was mottled with odd white striations. His mouth twisted in a hungry leer, and even his teeth seemed sharper, more pointed, more animal-like. He looked like an evil caricature of himself.

In my split second of uncertainty, of dismay, Selene struck.

"An nahl nath rac!" she cried, and shot a bolt of crackly blue lightning toward Hunter. It hit his throat and he gagged, his eyes wide, and sank to his knees.

"Hunter!" I yelled. He still looked different, evil, and I knew Selene was doing it, but I couldn't help feeling repelled. I felt intense guilt and shame. I was supposed to trust myself, my own instincts, but the problem was, my instincts had been wrong before.

Now Selene was muttering dark spells as she advanced on me, and involuntarily I took a step back. All at once panic came crashing down on me: I had screwed up. I had made a good start but had lost it. Now Hunter was down, Mary K. was vulnerable, and I was going to die.

I felt the first prickles of Selene's spells as they flitted around me like biting insects. Tiny stings bit my skin, making me writhe, and gray mist swirled at the edges of my vision. I realized she was going to wrap me in a cloud of pain and smother me. And I couldn't stop her.

"Not my daughter."

I heard the Irish-accented voice clearly in my head, its sweet inflection not hiding the steel underneath the words. I recognized it instantly as Maeve, my birth mother. "Not *my* daughter," she said again in my mind.

I gulped in a breath. I couldn't let Selene win. Hunter was curled on the floor, motionless. I couldn't even see Mary K.; the gray mist had closed in so that I could see only Selene, glowing in front of me as if she contained a fire within her. In my mind I stretched out my hand to seize power, to draw it to me. I tried to forget everything, to concentrate only on my own spells of protection and binding. I am made of magick, I told myself. All of magick is mine for the taking. Again and again I repeated these words until they seemed part of my song, my chant that calls power. Ancient words, recognizable but unknown, came to my lips, and I flung out my arms and twirled in a circle, barely feeling my hair flying out in back of me.

"Menach bis," I muttered, feeling the words coming to me in a voice that I didn't recognize, a man's voice. Could it be Angus? "Allaigh nith rah. Feard, burn, torse, menach bis." I swirled faster in my circle of one, weaving this spell, this one perfect spell that would protect me, stop Selene, help Hunter, and keep Mary K. safe. To me it was like seeing a perfect geometric shape forming in space: the lines of the spell, its forms, its intersections and boundaries and limitations. It was a shape made of light, of energy, of music, and I saw it forming around me in the room, being woven by the words that spilled from my mouth.

And as the shape formed, I saw another shape come into focus in the background, behind Selene. Cal. He stepped through the door, into the library, and Selene's head turned toward him.

"Mother." His voice was clear, strong, but I couldn't read his intentions from his tone. Had he come to help me? Or to help Selene kill me?

No time to stop and ask. I saw myself as if from outside, dressed in Maeve's green silk robe, its hem rippling around my bare ankles like seawater as I turned. Magick crackled all around me, glowing like fireflies, floating in the air: a dandelion flower of magick that had burst and was seeding itself everywhere. Motes of power began to draw themselves around Selene. Inside me was a fierce pride, an exhilaration in my strength and the ecstasy of weaving this spell. With my ancient words I gathered the motes around Selene; I began to encase her in them, as if I were sealing her inside.

Dimly I realized what I was doing. Dimly I recognized the cage of ice and light as I wove it around Selene. It was the same as the cage that had imprisoned Maeve and Angus. But I had no time, no energy to spare for wondering what this meant, where this knowledge had come from. I was caught in the magick. It consumed me.

It was the most beautiful and the most terrifying thing I had ever seen. It was like the beauty of a star's death when it goes nova: exhilarating and devastating. The awe inside me welled up and spilled out of my eyes as tears: purifying salt crystals in and of themselves.

"No!" Selene bellowed suddenly, a horrible, gut-wrenching howl of fury and darkness. "No!" The crystal cage around her shattered, and she loomed within it, dark and malevolent and cloaked with blackness.

I didn't have the experience to duck or swerve or throw up a block. I saw the boiling cloud of dark vapor spinning away from Selene, churning toward me, and I knew that in a moment I would experience the soul being sucked from my body. All I could do was watch.

And then a dark form blocked my sight, and like a high-speed camera, my mind snapped image after image but gave me no time to process what happened. Cal surged forward, his eyes burning and hollow as he blocked Selene's attack on me. I stepped back, eyes wide, mouth open in shock as Cal absorbed the dark vapor; it surrounded him, fell upon him, and then he was sinking to the ground, his eyes already unseeing as his soul left his body.

Now I knew. He had come to help me.

Selene was on him in an instant, screaming, falling onto his chest, beating him, trying to force life back into him as I watched stupidly and without comprehension.

"Sgàth!" she shrieked, barely sounding human. "Sgàth! Come back!" I had never heard a banshee, but that's what she sounded like, an inhuman keening and wailing that seemed to have the agony of the world in it. Her son was dead, and she had killed him.

When Hunter staggered to me and grabbed my hand, I could only stare at him. He looked like himself again, pale and ill, but the Hunter I knew.

"Now," he croaked, his voice sounding charred. "Now."

It all came back to me again, my brain began to function, and Hunter and I took advantage of Selene's grief and joined our powers to bind her.

Feeling cold, I gathered my magick and wove it tightly once more, a beautiful cage. Hunter stepped forward and snapped the silver braigh onto Selene's wrists, catching her unguarded as she held Cal's face and wept over him. She screamed again, the chain already burning her flesh. I shrank back at the horror of it: Cal's dead body, Selene's grief, her endless screaming as she thrashed, trying to get the braigh off.

Then she paused for an instant, her eyes rolling back into her head, and began a deep guttural chant. I saw the silver chain begin to crumble and dissolve. "Morgan!" Hunter yelled, and quickly I dropped my beautiful cage of light and magick over her.

It was like watching a black moth slowly smothering inside a glass. Within a minute Selene's rage was burning out: her screams were quieting, her thrashing had stilled; she lay coiled inside my spell as if trying to hide from the pain.

When I met Hunter's eyes, he looked horrified, shaken, yet there was an acknowledgment on his face that at last he had accomplished his goal. He was breathing hard, sweat beading his pale face, and he met my eyes. "Let's get out of here," he said shakily. "This place is evil."

But I was frozen, staring at Cal. Beautiful Cal, whom I had kissed and loved so much. Kneeling, I reached out to touch his face. Hunter didn't try to stop me.

I shuddered and shrank back—Cal's skin was already cooling. Suddenly racking sobs began to burst through my chest. I wept for Cal: for the brief illusion of love that I'd cherished so deeply, for the way he'd given his own life for mine, for what he could have been if Selene hadn't warped him.

What happened then is hard to explain. Hunter shouted suddenly and I whirled, tears still raining down my cheeks, to see Selene standing, her wrists held in front of her. I could see the blisters, but the silver braigh was gone. Her golden eyes seemed to burn through us. Then she sank down, collapsing on the oriental carpet with her eyes closed. Her mouth opened, and a vaporous stream floated out, like smoke.

Hunter shouted again and threw out his arm to push me back. We watched as the vapor streamed upward and seemed to disappear through the one library window. Then it was gone, and Selene was still and ashen. Hunter stepped quickly to her and put his fingers against her throat. When he looked up, his eyes reflected his shock. "She's dead."

"Goddess," I breathed. I had helped kill Selene—and Cal, too. I was a murderer. How could Hunter and I be standing in a room with two corpses? It was incomprehensible.

"What was that smoke?" My voice was thin and shaky.

"I don't know. I've never seen anything like it before." He looked worried.

"Morgan?" came Mary K.'s voice, and I shook off my paralysis and hurried to her. She was sitting up, blinking, and then she stood to brush off her clothes. She looked around her as if she were waking from a dream, and maybe she was. "What's going on? Where are we?"

"It's all right, Mary K.," said Hunter in his still-raspy voice. He came and took her arm so that we braced her on either side. "Everything's all right now. Let's get you out of here."

By keeping his body close to her, Hunter managed to steer Mary K. out of the room without her seeing Selene's or Cal's bodies. I followed them, forcing myself not to look back. When we were in the hall, Hunter spelled the library door so that it couldn't be shut again. Then we went outside, into the darkness, the biting cold of winter pressing in on us.

As we came down the stone steps, Sky pulled up in her car, followed by a gray sedan. A stout man with graying hair climbed out, and Hunter moved to speak to him: he had to be the closest council member.

I sat on the broad stone steps in my gown. I couldn't think about what had just happened. I couldn't process it. All I could do was hold Mary K.'s hand and start to think up what I would tell my parents. Every version I could think of started with, "It's because I'm a witch."